We hope you enjoy this book.
Please return or renew it by the due date.
You can renew it at **www.norfolk.gov.uk/libraries**

Adam Cece lives in Adelaide with his family. He has always liked wondering about weird things, so he decided to write a book about a place where the very weirdest things happen.
adamcece.com

Andrew Weldon is a cartoonist based in Melbourne. He has written and illustrated several books for children.
andrewweldon.com

Adam Cece

illustrated by
Andrew Weldon

TEXT PUBLISHING MELBOURNE AUSTRALIA

textpublishing.com.au

The Text Publishing Company
Swann House
22 William Street
Melbourne Victoria 3000
Australia

First published by The Text Publishing Company, 2018.

Book design by Imogen Stubbs.
Illustrations © Andrew Weldon.
Typeset by J&M Typesetters.

Printed and bound in Australia by Griffin Press, an Accredited ISO AS/NZS 14001:2004 Environmental Management System printer.

ISBN: 9781925603484 (paperback)
ISBN: 9781925626520 (ebook)

A catalogue record for this book is available from the National Library of Australia.

This book is printed on paper certified against the Forest Stewardship Council® Standards. Griffin Press holds FSC chain-of-custody certification SGS-COC-005088. FSC promotes environmentally responsible, socially beneficial and economically viable management of the world's forests.

For Emma and Thomas.
Embrace uniqueness.
Cherish nonsense.
Stay wonderful.

1

The Capital of New Zealand

Kipp Kindle always knew his family wasn't like other families. They were weird—in fact, they were probably the weirdest family on Earth. It was just as well they lived in the town of Huggabie Falls, because Huggabie Falls was the weirdest place on Earth.

Take Mrs Turgan, for example, the teacher who was also a witch. Then there was the factory that existed in another dimension, the bottomless river, the topless hill, the train tunnel to nowhere, and the fact that every Sunday it got dark at four-thirty in the afternoon and every other day it got dark at eight—weird, weird, weird.

On top of all the usual weird things that happened in Huggabie Falls, one day an extremely weird thing happened. It was by far the weirdest thing that had ever happened anywhere. It was so weird that someone should write a book about it. In fact, somebody has. You are reading it.

Kipp Kindle didn't read this book to find out about the extremely weird thing that happened in Huggabie Falls. He heard about it at school.

His teacher, Mrs Turgan, was late again. She was supposed to be teaching mathematics that morning. Mathematics can be quite fun, but not if it's being taught to you by an actual witch. Mrs Turgan wore a black pointy hat. She had a big hairy wart on the end of her crooked nose, and a bumper sticker on her broomstick that read: Honk if you want to get turned into a newt!

Mrs Turgan's classroom was more like a dungeon than a classroom. If you were a student in Mrs Turgan's class, which unfortunately Kipp and his two best friends, Cymphany Chan and Tobias Treachery, were, then you were often too scared to lift the lid of your school desk. Inside you could find a thick book on geometry, but you were equally likely to encounter a deadly snake or a large, hungry tarantula.

However, on the day the extremely weird thing happened in Huggabie Falls, there was one student who waited eagerly for the mathematics lesson to start, and who happily risked being attacked by a desk-dwelling tarantula if it meant getting his hands on a tantalising geometry book. And that student was Ug Ugg.

Ug Ugg loved mathematics, which wasn't that weird, except for the fact that Ug was an eleven-year-old troll, and trolls don't usually like mathematics—trolls don't usually like anything other than clubbing things. Ug didn't even own a club, but he owned fourteen calculators, much to the shame of his entire troll family.

Now, where was I? Oh, that's right, Mrs Turgan was running late.

Ug Ugg was sitting in front of Kipp and Tobias, who were sitting in front of Cymphany. He turned around and frowned.

'I do hope Mrs Turgan isn't away sick today. We're supposed to be doing decimals. I could hardly sleep last night I was so excited.'

Kipp stared at Ug for a moment. He wondered what sort of peculiar creature got excited about decimals. He raised his eyebrows at Tobias.

If you saw Kipp Kindle and didn't know he was from one of the weirdest families in all of Huggabie Falls, you would think he was just an ordinary school kid, with a cheeky, up-to-no-good grin on his face, sneakers that spent more time on desks and tables than on the ground, and hair that looked like a rolling wave surging off his forehead.

'Let's hope Mrs Turgan is away sick today,' Kipp said. 'Maybe we'll get a nice friendly

substitute teacher, who isn't a master of the dark arts and who doesn't have blood-sucking bats for pets.'

Cymphany looked up from her book. 'Terrible Turgan is here today,' she said.

Cymphany Chan always wore her hair in a tight ponytail, yet somehow strands of it always managed to break free and tangle themselves around her glasses. She permanently had an expression on her face like she was eager to correct people, which of course she always was. In preparation for correcting people, she had learnt every known fact in human history. If you wanted to know what the average wingspan of a Peruvian white-striped pelican was, then Cymphany was the person to ask.

'I saw her,' Cymphany continued, 'up in the vulture's nest before school.'

Tobias gulped.

The vulture's nest was Kipp, Tobias and Cymphany's nickname for Mrs Turgan's office, because it was high up in the school's old clock tower, where only Mrs Turgan, on her broom, could get to it.

A wide smile spread across Ug's face. 'She's here. Oh, good. That's a relief.'

'A relief?' Tobias Treachery said. Tobias had black hair, black clothes and even his eye colour was black. But his face was pearl white, and that was probably because he was more scared of Mrs Turgan than anyone. 'Ug, Mrs Turgan is a maniac,' Tobias said. 'No one would actually want her to come to class.'

Now if Mrs Turgan had never shown up that day this would be the end of this story, after only a few pages, and no one is going to want a book they can finish reading in less than two minutes. So I am very relieved to inform you that Mrs Turgan was not sick, and that she did show up to teach Kipp, Tobias and Cymphany, and Ug, one second later.

She came swooping in the doorway, her black cloak flowing behind her, and the terrified children scrambled back to their seats.

She carried a big jar under her arm—a big jar containing a giant toad. And that giant toad looked rather dismayed.

Mrs Turgan slammed the jar down on her desk. 'This, children, is my husband,' she announced. She said husband as if to say, the selfish man who has made my life a misery for the last twenty years. 'Last night I cooked him his last roast dinner, and for the last time he said my cooking was ordinary. Now he is a toad, literally, which is funny, considering I've always thought of him as one anyway. Now, he no longer eats roast dinners—he eats only cockroaches and flies.'

Mrs Turgan glared at the class with her beady, witchy eyes. 'And any children who have not completed their homework will soon become those very cockroaches and flies.'

To say the children rushed up to the front of the class to hand in their homework would be like saying it is only slightly warm in the middle of an erupting volcano. Many children were almost seriously injured in the frantic stampede to Mrs Turgan's desk. And those who had not completed their homework—which was certainly not Ug or, as it happened, Kipp, Tobias or Cymphany—slipped out of the classroom via the back door as quickly as they could, hoping Mrs Turgan would not spot them and see to it that they ended up in her husband's green belly.

When everyone who hadn't left sat back down, Mrs Turgan removed her black pointy witch's hat and dropped it onto her desk. It landed next to a bubbling cauldron of marinated bats' tongues, which smelled like old smelly socks that have been sprayed with old-smelly-sock odour enhancer. Mrs Turgan adjusted her robes and raised one bushy, disgusted eyebrow at the fidgeting children in front of her.

After a long pause, Mrs Turgan said calmly, 'Who knows something about the extremely weird thing that happened in Huggabie Falls?'

Now, when a normal person in a normal town talks of something weird happening, it's usually not all that weird and people say, 'Oh, is that all?' as if to say, weird things happen all the time, the world is full of weirdness, there is no need to get excited. But if a witch who is a teacher talks about something *extremely* weird happening then you know it must be something extremely, extremely weird.

Kipp glanced at Tobias and Cymphany. They both looked back at him and shrugged their shoulders.

'Kipp Kindle,' snarled Mrs Turgan. 'You always look suspicious, you obnoxious trouble-maker, but you look particularly suspicious now.'

Kipp jumped. His cheeky grin was gone and he was suddenly frozen with fear at the sight of the angry witch, who only last week had turned Benedict Bott into a pumpkin, and the poor boy had been sitting on the classroom windowsill rotting ever since.

'Honestly, Mrs Turgan,' Kipp said. 'I don't know anything about the extremely weird thing that has happened.'

Mrs Turgan reached inside her robes, which is where, as everyone knew, she kept her wand. She had that look in her eye as if she was having the delicious thought of turning someone into a camel, when she noticed timid Henrietta Humpling's raised hand.

'What is it, Miss Humpling?' Mrs Turgan sighed, in a way that indicated she was upset at having her malicious and wonderful thoughts of turning Kipp into a camel interrupted.

Henrietta Humpling was eleven. She was one-third vampire, one-third werewolf and one-third Dutch. 'Mrs Turgan, what is this extremely weird thing that has happened?' she asked.

An evil sneer spread across Terrible Turgan's face. 'You'll find out soon enough, you unfortunate little girl. In fact, all you wretched children will soon find out what the extremely weird thing that has happened is. Now, I must continue with my broth. I can't waste my time teaching mathematics at a time like this.'

A large disappointed frown dropped across Ug's face, but then Mrs Turgan added, 'Ug will take the rest of the class.'

Ug was overjoyed with this prospect, and with his size-eighteen feet and gargantuan grin he made his way clumsily to the front of the class.

Ug pulled down the whiteboard, revealing a sentence that read:

The capital of New Zealand is Wellington, not Auckland as most people think.

Which was an unusual thing to find, as there was no geography lesson this morning. But so many things in Huggabie Falls were weird, so Ug wiped it off and proceeded to write on the whiteboard such advanced algebra that Albert Einstein would have had scratched his head in bewilderment.

Ug's algebra was so torturous, in fact, that the children were almost relieved when Mrs Turgan's broth exploded and everyone had to evacuate the classroom as quickly as possible.

2

Definitely Not a Pirate

If you ever want to find out about something that has happened in Huggabie Falls—say, if you were three inquisitive children who had just been told of an extremely weird occurrence by your teacher, who also happens to be a witch— then your first port of call should be the home of old Mr Harold Haurik, because no one knows more about the goings on in Huggabie Falls than gruff, unshaven Harold Haurik, with his wooden leg and his eye patch.

You might be surprised to learn that Mr Haurik has no pirate ancestry, despite his pirate-like appearance. In fact, he will object strongly to any suggestion that he resembles those 'murderous scavengers o' th' seas', as he calls pirates. But, even though he wasn't a pirate, Mr Haurik did possess treasure, not of the buried variety, but rather the treasure of knowledge.

On the day that the extremely weird thing happened in Huggabie Falls, it was this treasure that Kipp, Tobias and Cymphany desperately needed. So, after they'd evacuated their class-room, they went to visit Mr Haurik, who lived in a caravan on the shore of the bottomless lake.

Mr Haurik's caravan had started out as a standard one, until he decided to increase the height of the interior ceiling to accommodate the parrot he had recently purchased to sit on his shoulder. Further minor renovations followed, and before long Mr Haurik's tiny caravan had become a four-storey, eight-bedroom mansion, with a six-car garage, an undercover swimming

pool and a rooftop tennis court, all of which could be towed behind an ordinary motor car.

'Ahoy, me hearties,' called Mr Haurik, who was sitting, fully clothed for some strange reason, in one of his caravan's three hot-tub spas. 'To what do I owe yer visit?'

It would have looked quite weird to any passer-by—a man who looked like a pirate, with a parrot perched on his shoulder, sitting fully clothed in a spa out the front of a four-storey caravan, talking to three children wearing school uniforms that were covered in bits of marinated bats' tongue from a recently exploded cauldron. Then again, any passer-by who lived in Huggabie Falls would think nothing of it—this was Huggabie Falls after all.

'You shouldn't put your wooden leg in the water, Mr Haurik,' warned Cymphany, as she and Kipp and Tobias walked across the caravan's gangplank. 'The wood will rot, unless you've got some waterproof varnish on it or something.'

Mr Haurik looked down at his submerged

limb. 'I can't stand me wooden leg anyways. People keep mistakin' me for one o' those murderous scavengers o' th' seas!'

'A pirate?' said Cymphany. 'I can't imagine why people would mistake you for a pirate.' She smiled, as if to say, perhaps it's not just the leg but the eye patch, the parrot and the alarming amount of pirate talk you are always using.

Mr Haurik moved his eye patch to his other eye. 'Young Cymphany Chan, be that ye, lass? And bless me barnacles, if that isn't scallywag Tobias Treachery. Ye have grown since I last saw ye. And Kipp Kindle, how be yer poor ol' mum and dad?'

Kipp looked uneasy when Mr Haurik mentioned his parents. 'We're here to find out about the extremely weird thing that has happened in Huggabie Falls, Mr Haurik. Can you tell us what it is?' Kipp was often embarrassed by his family, because they were so weird, even by Huggabie Falls' particularly weird standards.

'No one at school could tell us, and Mrs

Turgan won't tell us,' said Kipp, as if to say, nasty old witches like Mrs Turgan take great joy in keeping secrets from children they despise. 'But everyone's talking about what it could be.'

With the mention of the extremely weird thing that had happened, Mr Haurik launched himself from the hot tub, sending bucket-loads of water into the air so they rained down over Kipp, Tobias and Cymphany. Now the three children were soaking wet with Mr Haurik's grimy spa water and Mrs Turgan's marinated bats' tongues. All things considered, they would have preferred not to be soaked in either.

'Ye mean ye don't be knowin' nothin' about th' extremely weird thing that's happened?' Mr Haurik hollered, shaking his fists in the air and making his dripping-wet jacket sleeves flap water everywhere. 'This town and its wicked secrets.'

'Secrets, secrets, wicked secrets,' squawked Mr Haurik's parrot.

'I should get me cutlass and slay that barnacle-covered Turgan for not tellin' ye kiddies th' truth straightaway, especially ye, young Kindle, as it affects ye so.'

'Affects me?' Kipp blinked. 'What is it, Mr Haurik?' Kipp asked, as if to say, just tell us what's going on, would you? We can't handle the suspense any longer.

Now Harold Haurik knew what the extremely weird thing that had happened was, and he would have told the children right then, if not for the loud ding of his oven timer sounding at that very moment.

Mr Haurik's ears pricked up, as did his parrot's, if parrots even have ears, which I assume they must because they seem to hear things. '*Arrr!*' Mr Haurik said. 'That'll be me muffins. I've got to make up me icin' now and draw little skulls and crossbones on top o' them. Then ye sprogs'll be helping me eat th' tasty morsels, I imagine.'

Mr Haurik turned to go inside.

'Mr Haurik?' Kipp tugged at Mr Haurik's jacket, as if to say, aren't you forgetting something? 'What about the extremely weird thing that has happened?'

Mr Haurik turned back, blocking out the sun. His face was suddenly dark and eerie. He loomed over Kipp like someone, flyswatter in hand, might loom over a tiny fly.

'Run home, Kipp Kindle. Ye may want to scamper in the other direction rather than face th' great horror that awaits ye there, but ye must go. Ye and yer friends need to sort out this extremely weird thing that has happened. Huggabie Falls is dependin' on ye. Could happen to me next. Could happen to all o' us.'

Then, as if someone switched a switch inside Mr Haurik from fearful back to cheerful, he returned to the topic of muffins. 'Now me stomach be cryin' out for a feast o' banana and walnuts. Inside we go to me grand dinin' room, me hearties.'

But would you want to stick around and eat banana-and-walnut muffins cooked by a man who is not a pirate who has just told you about a great horror awaiting you at home that has something to do with an extremely weird thing that has happened? No, of course you wouldn't. I was in exactly the same situation last week, except that the muffins were chocolate, not banana-and-walnut, and let me tell you I didn't hang around to eat a single one. Neither did Kipp, Tobias and Cymphany. They were already halfway down the street before Mr Haurik had even finished his sentence about going inside.

'You don't suppose it's anything too serious, do you?' Tobias said as they ran.

'I don't know,' Kipp replied as best he could, while running as fast as he could. 'I don't want to spend time discussing it. I just want to find out what *it* is as soon as possible.'

'Wait a minute,' yelled Cymphany, sliding to a stop as though she'd just run into in a large puddle of glue.

Kipp and Tobias screeched to a stop too. 'What?' they said in urgent unison.

Cymphany shrugged. 'I forgot to tell

Mr Haurik that Roseau is the capital of Dominica, an island in the Caribbean, which I thought Mr Haurik might be interested in, seeing as there used to be a lot of pirates in the Caribbean.'

Tobias frowned. 'What is it with you and capital cities, Cymphany?' You wrote that capital city sentence on the whiteboard, didn't you?'

Cymphany shrugged. 'I just like them, that's all.'

Tobias looked confused. 'You like capital cities?'

Kipp, on the other hand, had no time for confusion. He had already started running again, realising that right now talk of capital cities was far less important than getting home.

'You're weird, Cym,' said Tobias, and he ran off after Kipp.

Cymphany looked quite pleased with herself, as if she wanted nothing more than to be at least a little bit weird, which of course she did.

And then she ran off after her friends.

3

The Business Card

Despite his name, Tobias Treachery was one of the most loyal friends anyone could ever have. This could not be said for the rest of the Treachery family, who lived their lives, as their family name would suggest, as dishonestly and disloyally as humanly possible.

So widespread was the Treachery family's treachery that there was not one person in all of Huggabie Falls who had not been a victim of a treacherous Treachery family act. This had earned the Treachery family a reputation as the most disliked family in all of Huggabie Falls. So it was no surprise that the Treacherys had to barricade the doors and windows of their house with planks of wood to keep the endless stream of revenge-seekers out.

All of this meant that Tobias had a mild vitamin D deficiency from the lack of sunlight finding its way into his house, and he didn't have many friends at school, or, to be more accurate, it meant he didn't have *any* friends at school. Until Kipp Kindle moved to Huggabie Falls. Kipp's family was the weirdest family ever, and so he didn't have any friends at school either, so Tobias and Kipp had that in common. Before long they became best of friends and, subsequently, Tobias spent a lot of time at the Kindles' house. Tobias really liked the Kindles' house, especially the fact that it had no wooden boards over the windows, which meant the rooms were always full of sunlight, and the indoor plants didn't die all the time.

Tobias spent so much time at the Kindles' house that you could say it had become his second home. In fact, he spent so much time you could say it had become his second, third, fourth and fifth homes.

It was due to the fact that Tobias considered himself an honorary Kindle that Mr Haurik's ominous warning that something terrible was happening to the Kindles created a rising ball of panic in Tobias's stomach, which spurred him to run faster than he ever knew he could.

However, when Tobias, Kipp and Cymphany arrived at 1778 Digmont Drive, the home of the Kindles, Kipp held up his hand to stop his friends.

'I have to go in alone,' Kipp said. 'And face whatever horror lies within—it's my house, after all. You and Cymphany needn't also be subjected to it.' For all Kipp knew, the great horror might be dangerous. People don't often talk of great horrors when they are describing gentle and completely non-dangerous things.

Tobias and Cymphany were quite upset by Kipp's order. Cymphany, like Tobias, had spent so much time at the Kindles' house that it was like a second home to her, too. When Cymphany had first moved to town she didn't have any friends, due to the fact that her family was the most normal family in all of Huggabie Falls. It was ironic that Cymphany was an outcast due to her family being so normal, while

Kipp was an outcast because his family was so weird. But Cymphany was lucky to become an outcast, because she became friends with Kipp and Tobias as a result, and in them she found a couple of loyal and wonderful companions.

So Cymphany was just as worried about Kipp's family as Tobias was, and only after a period of whining, did she and Tobias reluctantly agree to wait outside. They plonked themselves down on the footpath while Kipp prepared to face the unknown situation inside his house, alone.

With a gulp of courage Kipp approached the front door, the words of Mr Haurik still echoing in his mind—*th' great horror that awaits ye there.*

Now, as the storyteller, I should warn you that what Kipp is about to see when he enters his house is unbelievably scary, and anyone reading this who suffers from either a nervous disorder or a heart condition should put this book down immediately. I cannot take any responsibility for any insane fright suffered, or subsequent emotional trauma endured, if you, the reader, make the conscious decision to keep on reading at this point.

Wait a minute, what am I saying? I seem to be a little confused, because this book is *The Extremely Weird Thing that Happened in Huggabie Falls*, not *The Unbelievably Scary Thing that Happened in Huggabie Falls*. An unbelievably scary thing did happen in Huggabie Falls once, but I can't imagine why anyone would ever want to write a book about that. How silly of me. It must have been Mr Haurik's exaggerated talk of a great horror. What Kipp was about to see was not unbelievably scary, at least not to you and me, so I must apologise, and you can feel free to read on at your leisure.

Kipp opened his front door.

'Shocked' is not nearly strong enough a word to describe what Kipp felt when he saw his home. It's akin to using the word 'minor' to describe a head-on collision between a truck carrying a load of dynamite and a truck carrying a load of matches. But there really is no single word that adequately describes the complete and utter amazement and disbelief that a person feels when they look upon an incomprehensibly weird scene, so 'shocked' will have to do for now.

Kipp's father sat, legs crossed, in his big brown leather armchair, with a copy of the *Huggabie Falls Gazette* open in front of him. As the door shut, he said, 'Kipp, my boy, how was school today?' He looked his son up and down, and his moustache twitched. 'Good lord, you look out of breath, and you're wet! You look as though you've been soaked in hot-tub spa water and is that'—he sniffed the air—'the smell of marinated bats' tongues?'

Despite Kipp's shock, he had to be impressed by his father's astounding olfactory accuracy.

'What have you been up to?' Mr Kindle asked, as if to say, I can't imagine any activity that would involve you smothering yourself in marinated bats' tongues and then climbing into a spa, fully-clothed.

But Kipp didn't respond to his father's question. He was too busy staring, mouth agape. In the background, his younger sister Kaedy sat crossed-legged on the lounge-room floor, watching cartoons.

'I know,' Kaedy said, without taking her eyes off the television. 'They're normal. It's weird. Get over it.'

Kipp's mother strolled into the room, holding wet-clay-covered hands out in front of her. The sound of a pottery wheel winding down could be heard coming from the other room—it may not surprise you to learn that Mrs Kindle had recently started attending pottery classes.

'I thought I heard the door. Hello, dear.' She stopped and wiped her hands down her apron, upon which were the words 'Kiss the Cook', although it would have been more appropriate if the words upon it were 'Kiss the Potter'. As she wiped her hands, one eyebrow went up at Kipp. 'Why do you smell of marinated bats' tongues?'

'I've already asked him that,' said Kipp's father. 'And he just stands there staring at me like a fish. He hasn't even blinked yet. A fly just flew into his mouth and he didn't even notice.'

Kipp's parents continued to stare at him, and Kipp continued to stare at them. It took him a full minute before he could even speak, he was so shocked, although we have already established that he was far more than shocked, but I still haven't thought of a better word so we'll just have to stick with shocked.

When Kipp finally found himself able to speak, all he could think to say was, 'What's happened to you? You're both so, so...'

Then it suddenly sank in. It was something Kipp had always yearned for, but now that it had unexpectedly happened it was not at all like he had imagined.

'...normal.'

Kipp's parents glanced at each other.

'Yes.' His mother smiled. 'It's awfully strange, isn't it? But what about you? You're acting very strangely, dear. Very...what's the word?'

'Weird?' suggested Kaedy.

'Yes.' Kipp's mother nodded. 'That's it, weird.'

Weird? *Weird*? Kipp could hardly believe the words coming out of his mother's mouth. His mother, one of the weirdest people in all of Huggabie Falls, second in weirdness only to his father, was calling *him* weird.

'Speaking of weird,' said Kipp's mother, as if she'd just remembered something. 'A letter came for you today from your friend, Cymphany.'

Kipp's mother pulled a piece of paper out of the front pocket of her apron. 'It's a letter that simply reads, "The capital of Brazil is Brasilia."' Kipp's mother looked up. 'What do you suppose that means? Brasilia? It's a bit odd for Cymphany to send a letter like that, isn't it? She used to be such a normal girl.'

'She's a looney,' Kaedy chimed in, still butting into the conversation without ever taking her eyes off the television screen.

Kipp didn't have time to wonder why Cymphany was obsessed all of a sudden with capital cities. Kipp was about to explode. He couldn't believe what his eyes and ears were telling him: his parents were normal. Kaedy may have been okay with it, because all she cared about was watching cartoons, but it was too much for Kipp and he ran screaming from the house.

Cymphany and Tobias, who were waiting on the footpath, heard Kipp screaming as he bolted down the driveway. They jumped up just before Kipp ran them over.

'What happened?' Cymphany's face was flooded with concern. 'Was it as horrible as Mr Haurik described?'

Kipp took a moment to catch his breath. 'Worse.'

'No,' said Tobias. He looked sick.

'They're normal!' Kipp said. 'My parents are completely normal.'

Cymphany and Tobias looked at each other, puzzled. 'So,' said Tobias, slowly. 'To clarify, everything's okay, then?' Tobias said it not so much as a question but more as a statement, as if to say, maybe they could just forget all this talk of an extremely weird thing now and concentrate on enjoying the rest of this sunny day.

'You don't get it,' said Kipp. 'They're n-o-r-m-a-l.'

'You mean—' said Cymphany.

'Yes.' Kipp nodded. 'Completely.'

'You mean they're not—' Cymphany started to say.

35

'No,' said Kipp.

It took a few seconds for this extraordinary information to sink in, and all three confused children said nothing for a short while.

Then Cymphany shook her head. 'But what does all this mean?'

'I don't know, but I will bet you it has something to do with this card,' said Tobias, holding up the card to which he was referring. 'I found it in your letterbox, Kipp.'

'I wondered what you were doing over there,' said Cymphany.

They all huddled around the small business card that Tobias held. The card read:

Dark's Weirdness Investigation and Eradication Agency

PROPRIETOR: FELONIOUS DARK
123 Digmont Drive, Huggabie Falls

I find weirdness and I remove it.

Free, no obligation quotes.

'Well,' said Kipp, as if to say, that is a rather conveniently placed clue, isn't it.

Now, you, as the reader, may suspect that I, as the writer, planted that business card in the Kindles' letterbox, just to keep this story moving along. But I didn't, I promise. I would never resort to such a despicable act of interference. Besides, I am not in the book so there is no way I could have planted it. I'll admit it is an amazing coincidence that it was there, in Kipp's letterbox, but I can hardly help that—coincidences happen, don't they? I am not the god of coincidences, I can't control them, so just leave me alone.

If we are quite finished with this business of god-of-coincidences accusations flying about, how about we get back on with the story?

Yes, good idea. I agree.

When Kipp, Tobias and Cymphany finished reading the card, Kipp said, 'It sounds like Dark's Weirdness Investigation and Eradication

Agency could definitely have been responsible for my parents turning normal all of a sudden. I mean look at this man's name for starters. Felonious Dark! Have you ever heard of a first name and a surname that don't begin with the same letter? That's very unusually weird.'

Sorry to interrupt again, but I just wanted to point out that if you, the reader, are the observant type then you will have already noticed that Mr Felonious Dark is the first character to appear in this book whose first name and surname don't begin with the same letter. If you haven't noticed this, well, I'm sorry to say you might not be the observant type, or you might sometimes be the observant type but were just a little bit out of form as you sailed through the first two and a half chapters of this book, blissfully unaware that you missed this fact, and probably many others. Or you might have noticed it, but put it down to an amazing coincidence, and although there are many amazing coincidences in Huggabie Falls—such as the business card in the letterbox—this is not one of them.

One of the many weird things about Huggabie Falls is that everyone who lives there has a first name and a surname beginning with the same letter. So the fact that Mr Felonious Dark's first name and second name started with different letters instantly makes him a highly suspicious character indeed.

This matching first name and surname thing is just another one of the many weird things about Huggabie Falls. If someone were so inclined, someone could write a whole book about how Huggabie Falls got to be so weird and how the many weird things came to be, and, now that I think about it, I very much intend to do that myself one day, but first I must finish this book, mustn't I.

Now, I seem to have become sidetracked again. Where was I?

Oh, that's right, I remember now.

As Kipp, Cymphany and Tobias discussed the unusually named Felonious Dark, and his weirdness investigation and eradication agency, Kipp's mum appeared on the front porch and sang out, 'Kipp, dear, come inside for dinner. No more playing with your friends now. I've made lasagne.'

It was now Tobias and Cymphany's turn to be shocked—I say 'shocked', of course, because I still haven't thought of a better word for their utter disbelief and amazement—at what they saw.

'First thing tomorrow we are going down to that weirdness investigation and eradication agency to demand some answers,' said Kipp. Cymphany and Tobias nodded in dumbfounded agreement. They couldn't take their astonished eyes off Mrs Kindle. They'd never seen her like this before.

'Look at her just standing there saying she's made lasagne for tea,' Kipp said, as if it was the most absurd thing ever, as if his mum had just come out and proclaimed she had built a rocket and was flying to Mars that evening.

'I know,' said Tobias. 'This is all just too weird, even for Huggabie Falls.'

Digmont Drive

For as long as Cymphany Chan could remember, her family had been the least weird family in all of Huggabie Falls.

Cymphany's father had only one weirdness, which was that he always stood slightly on a lean, as if he were attempting to impersonate the Leaning Tower of Pisa. Now, an askew stance is weird, that is undeniable, but it is such a minor weirdness that I wonder if it should really be classified as a weirdness at all.

Next, there was Cymphany's mother, who also had a weirdness about her that was sort of weird, in the way that vegetables with tomato sauce are sort of tasty. Cymphany's mother could read a whole novel in fifteen minutes, which was not so much a weirdness as something she had learnt to do in a twelve-week speed-reading course. Again, I wonder if this should be classified as a weirdness at all.

Last but not least, there was Cymphany's brother, Clark. Clark's weirdness, on the other hand, was weird: he could do backflips. Not so unusual, I hear you say—many people can do backflips. But Clark had been able to do them since he was one and a half hours old.

At the time of Clark's birth it was considered extremely weird. A picture of Clark doing backflips in his cot had even appeared on the front page of the *Huggabie Falls Gazette*, whose pages were only ever filled with stories and pictures of Huggabie Falls' weirdest people and places. It was a source of great pride for Cymphany's parents, who were highly disappointed by Cymphany's normalness. About the only weird thing about Cymphany was that she was afraid of heights, and even that was one of the most common, most unweird, things to be scared of.

Unfortunately, Clark never did display any further signs of weirdness. He'd moved away to college, and now, because the picture in the *Huggabie Falls Gazette* had started a baby-backflipping craze, many Huggabie Falls parents taught their babies to perform backflips before teaching them to crawl.

It didn't help, either, that Cymphany's family lived on a street that was home to some of

Huggabie Falls' weirdest families. There were the Kloveks, who were a family of happy elves, and whose house was an enormous Christmas tree, with each of their fourteen rooms contained inside enormous baubles. And the Tuggenmeisters, a family of inter-dimensional beings, whose house was upside down and inside out, so every time you entered it, you left it again and every time you looked up you saw down, which made hanging wall paintings quite impossible.

All these weird families living in the street only highlighted the fact that the Chans just weren't that weird, and all her life Cymphany had secretly wished for a family that was even a teeny bit more weird.

Funnily enough, on the opposite side of town, Kipp Kindle wished for a family that was a teeny bit more normal, or, at the very least, not the weirdest family ever to live in Huggabie Falls. And now, with the extremely weird thing that had happened in Huggabie Falls, his wish had suddenly come true. But while you would have thought Kipp would be happy about this, he wasn't. Instead, he had tossed and turned through a sleepless night. He wasn't sure why he was upset, and then he was even more upset that he was upset when he shouldn't be.

The evening before had been filled with normalness. The Kindles had eaten very normal lasagne for dinner, then watched some overly normal television, then brushed their teeth—while looking in a mirror! And finally, the most normal thing of all, as Kipp had kissed his parents goodnight, without even thinking about it, he had said, 'See you in the morning,' even though this was something he had never, ever said to them before.

When Kipp woke up the next morning, he had hardly slept a wink from worry, and big puffy bags had collected under his eyes. He desperately wanted his weird family back.

He dressed silently and quickly and made his way downstairs. As he snuck outside he saw his mother in the kitchen making herself a cup of tea in a wonky pottery cup. Kipp shuddered. This weirdness had to stop!

Out on the street, Tobias had been waiting for Kipp since dawn, and he, too, had droopy eyes.

'You couldn't sleep either?' Kipp asked. 'Is your family normal, too?'

'I wish,' said Tobias. 'Mr Yugel, the bank manager, spent all night pounding on our front door, demanding our family pay back the loan we took out from the Huggabie Falls Bank four years ago.' Tobias yawned and, because yawns are infectious, Kipp yawned too.

Tobias and Kipp didn't have to wait long for Cymphany to come bouncing down the street. She was eager to get cracking on solving the mystery of the extremely weird thing that had happened.

She was carrying her satchel. Cymphany was always carrying her satchel. As far as Kipp and Tobias knew, it was bottomless, as it seemed to contain something for every occasion. Today she removed from her satchel an assortment of detective items, including a pen and notebook for documenting the interview they were undoubtedly going to have with Mr Felonious Dark. Cymphany had also packed a torch, a junior-detective fingerprint kit and some chocolate-chip cookies, which had nothing to do with detective work but a lot to do with the fact that children love chocolate-chip cookies.

'Your parents aren't the only ones,' Cymphany said, reading the worried look on Kipp's face. 'Did you read the *Huggabie Falls Gazette* this morning?'

Kipp and Tobias shook their heads. 'We don't get the *Gazette* delivered anymore,' Tobias said, 'because we never paid our bill.'

'Well,' Cymphany continued, 'a lot of Huggabie Falls' weirdest people and weirdest things are suddenly turning normal, and no one can explain why. Mr Brumfoot, the man with the enormous hands, whose finger paintings are world-famous, woke up today with his hands shrunk right down to normal size. He's lost his livelihood overnight. And there are others. It seems almost every hour a new person loses their weirdness. And it's not just people. Someone found the top of the topless hill. Apparently, it was hidden under a bush. The town is in a panic. Everyone's worried about this wave of normality and who or what is going to be next.'

Cymphany grinned. 'It looks like my family will be the weirdest family in all of Huggabie Falls soon,' she said, as if to say, wouldn't that be ironic justice if everyone who has accused my family of being so terribly normal all these years suddenly became normal themselves?

'It must have something to do with Dark's Weirdness Investigation and Eradication Agency,' said Tobias. 'We have to find it as soon as possible.'

'We should skip school today,' Kipp said. 'I can't concentrate on school at a time like this. I just hope it's not too late to turn everything back to the way it was.' Kipp looked at his home as he said this, and he sighed.

'But what about Mrs Turgan?' Tobias said, grimacing. 'She hates truancy. Remember when Milo McFerny skipped class? They say she turned him into one of the toilet bowls on the second floor. Every time I use one of those toilets I wonder if I'm about to wee on poor Milo.

Cymphany shook her head. 'Turgan's always dangerous, whether or not we attend class, and we have to help Kipp.'

Tobias looked at Kipp's worried face and nodded. Tobias was a loyal friend, and his loyalty seemed to override his cowardice on this occasion. 'Okay, let's do it.' He gulped. 'First thing we have to do is find this weirdness investigation and eradication agency.'

At this point in the story, I should mention that I, as the storyteller, don't condone any children skipping school for any reason whatsoever. Obviously Kipp, Tobias and Cymphany thought that, considering the circumstances, it would be okay, just this once, to skip school. Parents of children reading this book would be horrified, I'm sure, if they thought for one moment that I encouraged this sort of behaviour, but then again parents of children reading this book would certainly understand that I am merely telling the story, *ipso facto* I cannot in any way control what Kipp, Tobias and Cymphany do. I can only report it.

Now, where was I?

Oh, that's right, the three school-skipping children, Kipp, Tobias and Cymphany, acting without the consent of me, the storyteller, soon found themselves searching for 123 Digmont Drive, the office of Dark's Weirdness Investigation and Eradication Agency.

I know you may be thinking here that I have incorrectly used the word searching. You may be thinking this because, according to the business card from chapter three, Dark's Weirdness Investigation and Eradication Agency is located at 123 Digmont Drive. And you may also have noticed, if you are one of the observant readers we talked about earlier, that the Kindles' house is located at 1778 Digmont Drive, so you have naturally assumed that these two locations are on the same (long) street. It was very silly of you to assume that. You have made this assumption by applying a rule applicable to any normal town, which is if two buildings are addressed as being on the same street then those two buildings will indeed be on the same street. But we have already established that Huggabie Falls is no normal town. It is a weird town, the weirdest town on Earth, in fact, and therefore normal-town rules do not apply.

There are more than one hundred streets, roads, alleys and groves in Huggabie Falls, and all of them are named Digmont Drive. As with many of the weird things about Huggabie Falls, which I will one day write a big book about, it has been a long time since anyone has even thought to question why this is so. Whatever the

reason, there is one major downside to living in a town where every street, road, alley and grove is named Digmont Drive, and that is the fact that addresses are basically useless.

Kipp, Tobias and Cymphany had the address of Dark's Weirdness Investigation and Eradication Agency, but they had no idea where to find it, or where to start looking.

'Well, we know all the roads and streets around our houses, around our school and on the way to Mr Haurik's caravan,' said Cymphany. 'And we know Dark's Weirdness Investigation and Eradication Agency isn't on any of those.'

'Maybe,' suggested Tobias, 'we should just start from one corner of town, perhaps over near the bottomless lake, and work our way all the way to the other side of town, where there's that banana tree that grows microwave ovens.'

'That's going to take us all day,' said Cymphany, wondering if she'd packed enough chocolate-chip cookies.

'Well then, we'd better get started,' said Kipp.
And so they did.

It took four long, muscle-wearying hours for the three school-skipping children to find Dark's Weirdness Investigation and Eradication Agency, at 123 Digmont Drive, which happened to be a small dishevelled stone building hidden away down a gritty alley beside the Huggabie Falls Public Library.

The children waited nervously in the cold and draughty waiting room of Dark's Weirdness Investigation and Eradication Agency, sitting on uncomfortable steel chairs and being eyed suspiciously by a large receptionist, who had purple curlers in her red hair and yellow stains on her teeth.

It was some time before she gave them an unpleasant grunt, as if to say, they could go in and see Mr Dark now, and she pointed towards a rickety wooden door, which hung ajar. The room beyond it was inky black.

Kipp, Tobias and Cymphany made their way through the door one by one, pushing cobwebs aside as they went.

'Nice place,' said Cymphany, as if to say, this place is scary and I'm not so sure we should be here at all.

Once inside the room, Cymphany, Tobias and Kipp stood in total blackness and silence, before the striking of a match interrupted both the blackness and the silence. The flame from the match illuminated the face of a thin, menacing-looking man.

The menacing-looking man didn't say anything, he just continued looking menacing.

Kipp took a gulp of courage. 'Mr Dark?' he asked.

The thin, menacing-looking man used the match to light two candles, which cast barely enough light for Kipp, Tobias and Cymphany to see that the man wore a pin-striped suit that was too tight even for his slim body, and that he sat at a dusty old desk with three child-sized

chairs positioned in front of it.

Kipp, Tobias and Cymphany exchanged looks, as if to say, that's very strange—was this menacing-looking man expecting us?

'I'm Mr Felonious Dark,' he said at last, although he didn't speak as such; he sort of hissed. 'Won't you sit down? Excuse the candlelight. I haven't been able to pay my electricity bill this month. Business has been a little slow, but I imagine with the extremely weird occurrences, it will soon pick up.' There was a glint of mischief in Felonious Dark's beady black eyes.

'Actually, that's what we're here about,' said Tobias.

A wry smile spread across Felonious Dark's pale face. 'Oh, yes?' He lifted his eyebrows a bit late, as though pretending the news was a surprise to him, whereas it was obvious it wasn't. 'You want to know something about the extremely weird thing that has happened, or, to be more accurate, that is still happening?'

The children peered at each other. Cymphany

rummaged in her satchel for her notebook, in order to take notes during the questioning of Felonious Dark they were about to commence. She soon realised, however, that notebooks are wonderful if there is actually enough light in the room to see what you are noting, which there is not by candlelight, so she stuffed her notebook away again, wishing she had thought to bring a miniature audio recording device.

Felonious Dark smiled. 'Why would you think I knew anything about the extremely weird thing that is happening?'

'Well, you must admit it is quite a coincidence,' said Cymphany, in an accusing tone, still a bit grouchy at herself for forgetting a recording device.

Felonious Dark chuckled. 'A coincidence?'

'Well, as you mentioned,' Cymphany said, 'something is eradicating all the weirdness from our town, at about the same time as the appearance of your new agency that claims to eradicate weirdness.'

Felonious Dark upped his chuckle to a cackle. 'I assure you, children, my agency is not new. I've been here for years. I simply change my agency's name depending on where the business is. The occurrence of these extremely weird things is the reason for my latest name change.'

'So,' Kipp said. 'How do you explain your business card being in my letterbox?'

Upon seeing the business card that Kipp held up, Felonious Dark upped his cackle to a guffaw. 'Ah, you must be the Kindle boy. Yes, I was at your house investigating the extremely weird thing that happened there, just like you have come here investigating the same matter. But I assure you I had nothing to do with your family's sudden bout of normality.'

'Do you expect us to believe that?' said Cymphany, getting a tad carried away.

'I expect,' said Mr Dark, suddenly slamming his hands down and standing up, making Kipp, Tobias and Cymphany all jump, 'that children should respect their elders.'

'But, what about your name?' Cymphany blurted out.

'My name?' Felonious Dark frowned at her.

'Well your first and second names don't start with the same letter,' Cymphany explained. 'That's not normal.'

With the mention of his unusual name, Felonious Dark's large brow began to crease, and the children suspected that he was about to get very angry, a suspicion that was quickly confirmed.

'I am about to get angry,' boomed Felonious Dark. 'You don't want to see me get angry. I do very unpleasant things when I'm angry.'

Kipp tensed, and his eyes darted across to Tobias, who had said nothing for a while. Tobias was staring at a book that sat on Felonious Dark's desk. In the weak candlelight Kipp could just make out the words on the cover:

HOW TO FOOL NOSEY CHILDREN
BY TRENT THACKERY

Kipp only had time to think, that's odd, before Tobias sprang to his feet. 'Well I think we've wasted enough of your time, Mr Dark, sir,' he said.

'We have?' Cymphany said, as if to say, this thin, menacing-looking man is obviously lying. We must question him some more.

'You have?' said Felonious Dark, alarmed.

'We have,' confirmed Kipp, and he and Tobias began to drag Cymphany from the office of Felonious Dark, under Felonious Dark's untrusting gaze.

They were ever so close to getting out of there when Felonious Dark boomed again, 'Aren't you forgetting something, Ms Chan?'

All three children stopped, a little stunned that Felonious Dark knew Cymphany's name.

Cymphany struggled free of Tobias's grip. 'Forgetting something?' she said.

Felonious Dark curled his thin lips into a cruel sneer. 'You haven't stated a capital city yet. You're running out of time? What about the

capital city of Panama, that's an easy one. Or...
perhaps you don't know it?'

'Of course I know it,' said Cymphany,
standing up straight. 'It's Panama City.'

'Good.' Felonious Dark nodded. 'Now run
along, children.' He waved them off with his
bony hand.

Kipp, Tobias and Cymphany needed no more
encouragement. They quickly exited through
the rickety door from whence they had come,
into the reception area. The large receptionist
snarled under her breath, as if to say, don't come
back.

'What's going on?' demanded Cymphany,
as they stumbled out into the bright sunlit alley.
'How did that strange man know about my
capital cities and, more importantly, why did we
leave all of a sudden like that? We'll never find
out what happened to your parents now, Kipp.'

Now, being the storyteller, I should know every
twist and turn of this funny little tale, but I was

just as surprised as you that Felonious Dark seemed to know of Cymphany's tendency to declare capital cities. More concerning to me though, was Felonious Dark's strange comment that time was running out, thus implying that he somehow knew this chapter was coming close to its conclusion. Of course, I am being ridiculous because for Felonious Dark to know such a thing would imply that he is somehow aware that he is a character in a book, but that is impossible. Characters are never aware of such things, even in Huggabie Falls. Nevertheless, I will have to keep an eye on Felonious Dark. So too will Kipp, Tobias and Cymphany.

Alas, I seem to have become sidetracked yet again. I really must stop doing that. Let us go back to the alley, shall we?

'Cymphany, the man was obviously lying,' said Tobias. 'Didn't you see the book on his desk? He had been expecting us all along. We're not going to get any answers from him. We're just going to get ourselves into danger.'

Cymphany stopped. 'Book?'

'Tobias is right,' said Kipp, and he told Cymphany about the book. 'The thing that puzzles me is why Felonious Dark left it on his desk. He must have known we'd see it, even in the dim light. Did he want us to know he was lying?'

Kipp, Tobias and Cymphany thought this over. Then Tobias sighed, and Kipp and Cymphany thought he had the answer, but he only had another question. 'What do we do now?' he asked.

'We wait,' suggested Cymphany. 'We wait for Felonious Dark to leave his office, and then we follow him.'

Kipp and Tobias agreed that this was an excellent plan, so the children hid behind a nearby tree and waited.

Unbeknownst to Kipp, Tobias and Cymphany, but knownst to me, somebody was watching them as they hid behind that tree.

It wasn't Felonious Dark, nor was it his large receptionist. It was somebody much worse. Soon that somebody-much-worse strolled up behind the children, without them noticing, and tapped one of them on the shoulder.

That one of them was Cymphany, and when they all turned around and saw who that somebody-much-worse was, they knew instantly they were in big trouble.

5

Ralph the Rat

The word petrified means paralysed with terror. For example a person who has a phobia of heights might be petrified to discover that they've been accepted into astronaut school.

Another example of petrified might be three children who have skipped school for the day to investigate an extremely weird thing that has happened, and who have suddenly run into their teacher.

Kipp, Tobias and Cymphany did not have a

phobia of heights, but they did have a phobia of their teacher, Mrs Turgan, who was peering down her hooked nose at them and smiling a mouthful of brown, crooked teeth.

'Well, well, well, what have we here?' said Mrs Turgan knowing full well that what she had here were three truant students, whom she could now to turn into lavatory seats, if she so desired.

'Kipp Kindle, Tobias Treachery and Cymphany Chan,' she said, as if to say, the three children soon to be known as toilet seat number one, toilet seat number two and toilet seat number three. 'Aren't you three supposed to be in school?'

'We're out on an excursion,' Cymphany squeaked.

'Funny,' said Mrs Turgan, and she put her finger to her chin in a pensive fashion. 'I was not aware of any excursions scheduled for today.' She said this with a sneer, as if to say, you'll have to do better than that you three little soon-to-be toilet seats.

'We're investigating the extremely weird thing that's happened,' said Cymphany, deciding that perhaps it would be best if they were honest.

A venomous smirk unfurled across Mrs Turgan's warty face. 'You should have stuck with your first story, Ms Chan. It was much more believable.'

She removed her wand from the pocket of her flowing black robes. The children were petrified at the sight of this magical instrument and considering the fact they were already petrified at the sight of Mrs Turgan, they now found themselves doubly petrified.

'I am going to enjoy this,' said Mrs Turgan. 'But you children most certainly will not. I haven't had the chance to punish any naughty children today. I was going to transform that irritating Bentley Booger boy into a slug of some description, but my wand got jammed.'

Mrs Turgan eyed her wand up and down with one wide, curious eye. 'It seems fine now. I'll test it, shall I?'

With that, Mrs Turgan raised her wand above her head, swished it downwards and screeched, *'Incantium Hippurum.'*

A blinding streak of purple flame erupted from the end of Mrs Turgan's wand and engulfed poor, shrieking Cymphany.

As people often do when confronted by searing flashes of magic purple flame, Kipp and Tobias shielded their faces. A second later they lowered their arms to see Mrs Turgan looking quite pleased with herself. And, in the space between them where Cymphany had stood only moments before, the purple smoke cleared to reveal a baby hippopotamus—a baby hippopotamus wearing Cymphany's glasses and satchel—with a rather surprised look on its plump little face.

'What have you done?' Kipp screamed at Mrs Turgan. 'You've turned Cymphany into'—he hesitated, as it was quite an unexpected development —'a baby hippopotamus!'

Mrs Turgan laughed. 'I certainly have, and

it was exactly what she deserved, firstly, for skipping school and, secondly, for trying to deceive me with ridiculous excuses.'

She glared at Kipp, who looked furious. 'I would think at this point you would be less worried about your friend's hapless fate and more worried about your own. My wand can bring about many more punishments for wicked children.'

Kipp looked at Tobias, in a what-are-we-going-to-do-now-we're-so-done-for-it's-not-funny? way.

Tobias looked back at Kipp in an I-know-it's-not-overly-helpful-right-now-but-I-told-you-we-shouldn't-have-skipped-school way.

Mrs Turgan began to raise her wand again. Tobias's eyes were clenched shut, but Kipp's eyes were darting.

Meanwhile, Cymphany was sitting with a rather perplexed look on her podgy grey face, staring at the two hoof-like feet that used to be her hands.

As Terrible Turgan's wand came down, thoughts were racing through Kipp's brain. He needed to think of something that would distract Mrs Turgan, something that would be more important to her than transforming vile children. The problem was that, as far as Kipp knew, transforming vile children was Mrs Turgan's absolute favourite thing to do.

Then, at the very last micro-second, Kipp thought of something.

'Mrs Turgan,' he said. 'Is that your husband over there?' He pointed. 'Why isn't he a toad anymore?'

'My husband,' screeched Mrs Turgan, as if to say, how did that despicable spouse of mine escape my toad transformation? She whipped her head around violently, following the line of Kipp's outstretched finger.

Mrs Turgan furiously surveyed the empty alley behind her. 'Where is he? I don't see that loathsome man anywhere.'

Once she realised she had been duped,

she turned back to see that this temporary distraction had given Kipp enough time to hoist his best friend, Cymphany, who was now a baby hippopotamus, onto his shoulders and start running for his life. She also saw that Kipp's other best friend, Tobias, was following closely behind.

Now, if you have ever tried to run from a witch while carrying a baby hippopotamus, as I myself have had to do on a number of occasions, you will appreciate how difficult it is. This is largely due to the fact that baby hippopotamuses, while being only babies, still weigh much the same as a full-grown anything else. Furthermore, a hippopotamus's weight is not evenly distributed throughout its body—it is focused in its sizeable belly region.

This sizeable belly region now sat atop Kipp's shoulders, which had never had to support much more than a school bag, and were not too happy about now being asked to transport a heavy aquatic mammal.

Tobias helped as best he could by holding some of Cymphany's weight from behind, but their progress was still quite slow, or to be more accurate it was painfully slow, and far from the quick getaway they were hoping for.

It didn't help that Mrs Turgan had the distinct advantage of being able to fly, via her broomstick. Within seconds, she hovered above the children, cackling at their futile attempt to flee.

Cymphany took matters into her own hooves. She leapt off Kipp's shoulders and began to run by herself. But she was not accustomed to running on four legs, never mind four hooves, and she ended up tumbling and somersaulting every few steps, whacking her snout painfully into the ground every time she did so. So Kipp hoisted her onto his shoulders again.

Kipp, Tobias and Cymphany made their way, inefficiently like this, out of Digmont Drive, where Dark's Weirdness Investigation and Eradication Agency was. They took a left onto

Digmont Drive, past the Huggabie Falls Public Library, and then took a right at Digmont Drive, near Ms Suddlehoney's Wish Shop. At the end of this Digmont Drive they turned right again into Digmont Drive, past the Huggabie Falls Imaginary Creatures Zoo. And all the time, brilliant flashes of purple flame crashed into the ground around them like fireworks as Mrs Turgan blasted viciously from above.

'You'll never escape, you wicked school-skipping children,' Mrs Turgan cackled, clearly enjoying the pursuit.

'We need to get indoors,' screamed Tobias as they ran. 'We need cover. If we get hit by one of those transforming bolts we're done for, and we'll never out run Mrs Turgan while she's on that broomstick.'

'Especially not while we have to lug a baby hippopotamus,' moaned Kipp.

Cymphany frowned. She was not at all happy about the fact that she had been turned into a baby hippopotamus, and the thought that

Mrs Turgan's transformation spell might be permanent was starting to concern her a great deal.

The only place the two children and one baby hippopotamus could seek refuge was, ironically, the place they should have been at to begin with: the Huggabie Falls Primary School. I wonder if there is some sort of message here about why children should not skip school, especially children who happen to have witches for teachers, but I wonder a lot of things, like, for instance, if Kipp, Cymphany and Tobias should have thought to turn left at Digmont Drive instead of right, because left was the way to the Huggabie Falls Sanctuary for People Fleeing from Witches and other Dangerous Flying Creatures.

Kipp, Tobias and Cymphany would wonder this themselves later on, but for now they wondered something else. They wondered why, in the middle of a school day, Huggabie Falls Primary School—with its twenty-one classrooms, five corridors, one science lab, one canteen, one sweaty-sock-smelling gymnasium and one oval with asteroid-proof grass—was completely deserted. They wondered this, but not for too long, as wondering about things for too long is a luxury afforded only to those not being pursued by flying witches.

So Kipp, Tobias and Cymphany darted into the first building they came to, which was the science building. Here, they hid in the cupboard under the stairs on the second floor, crammed in with brooms, old half-full paint cans and various pieces of scientific apparatus, including test tubes and Bunsen burners.

The cupboard was also home to Ralph, a laboratory rat, who, thanks to a bungled science experiment, could now speak Portuguese.

'*Bem, bem, bem, duas crianças e um hipopótamo, isso é muito estranho,*' exclaimed Ralph as Kipp, Tobias and Cymphany entered the cupboard.

Now, I, as storyteller, do not speak Portuguese, nor am I in possession of a Portuguese-to-English dictionary, so I can't even begin to guess what Ralph was saying. I gather it was something to do with a hippopotamus, as the word hippopotamus is obviously almost the same in Portuguese as it is in English, and maybe once I've finished writing this story I shall translate what Ralph said into English and include it in an additional section at the end of the book, but for now I really think I should get on with this climactic scene.

'Quiet, Ralph,' whispered Kipp. 'We're hiding from Mrs Turgan.'

'*Senhora Turgan*,' exclaimed Ralph. '*Eu tenho medo dela, eu ficarei quieto.*'

Again, I have no idea what Ralph was saying, and neither did Kipp, Tobias nor Cymphany, but they all assumed the word *quieto* meant Ralph was going to be quiet, so that was good enough for them.

Mrs Turgan did a few laps above the school, then set her broomstick down on top of grade-four teacher Mr Pottlebrush's award-winning rosebushes.

Once Mrs Turgan had made sure she'd completely trampled and flattened the rosebushes, she jumped off her broomstick and proceeded to patrol the lawns outside the science building like a lion stalking prey.

'I do not fancy the notion,' she shouted, 'of having to spend large amounts of time exploring all the hiding spots in the science building, looking for three troublesome children.'

A grin crept across her face. 'But what a silly duffer I am. I'm a witch, so I've got at my disposal many other less time-consuming ways to explore buildings.'

With that, Mrs Turgan scooped up a pile of small pebbles and tossed them high into the air. While the pebbles were still mid-flight she whipped out her wand, swished it and screamed, '*Incantium Nocturum.*'

A bolt of purple flame shot out of Mrs Turgan's wand and engulfed the airborne pebbles, only this time she did not transform them into baby hippopotamuses, but rather thousands of hungry vampire bats.

Mrs Turgan screeched with joy. 'A plethora of blood-sucking bats should do the trick.

They'll find those awful children soon enough,' she cackled.

On Mrs Turgan's command, the bats, like a swarm of demonic bees, flew across the lawns and burst through the doors of the science building. They flew in and out of classrooms, up stairs and along corridors, swooping and diving into every nook, frantically searching for tasty children to feast on.

None of the children or the baby hippopotamus, or the Portuguese-speaking rat, could see these bats from inside the cupboard, but they all soon heard the clawing and shrieking at the cupboard door. The children knew it wouldn't be long before the flying rodents would claw their way in.

'Oh no, they've found us,' Tobias sobbed. 'We're done for.'

Kipp glared at him. 'Not helpful, Tobias.'

'*Morcegos, morcegos, morcegos, morcegos horríveis*!' hollered Ralph and he scampered away into a nearby rat hole.

'If only we had a rat hole we could use to get away,' said Tobias, above the growing roar of even more bats now thrashing against the door.

Now you, as readers, might be very scared for Kipp, Tobias and Cymphany right now, as well you should be, for their lives are in mortal danger. I attended a nocturnal animals theme park with my parents when I was extremely young and naive, where a rather ignorant bat keeper, who claimed to be a bat expert, told me that bats were not dangerous creatures and that they would never intentionally harm human beings. I would very much like to see how long that dim-witted man would maintain his point of view if he were in that science building surrounded by thousands of Mrs Turgan's killer vampire bats.

Kipp, Tobias and Cymphany, unlike the misinformed bat keeper I once met, were under no illusion that the bats were harmless, and they knew they needed to find a way out of the second-floor science-building cupboard that didn't involve going out past thousands of pairs of merciless, sharp fangs.

Unfortunately, there didn't seem to be any other way out of the cupboard, unless you were rat-sized.

Tobias and Kipp looked at Cymphany, who stared back at them with her big baby-hippopotamus eyes. Maybe she would have been smart enough to come up with an escape plan, or maybe she had something in her satchel that could help them, but she wouldn't have been able to tell Kipp or Tobias about it, as neither of them were able to speak hippopotamus.

So all they could do was sit there and wait for the bats to scratch their way in.

$5\frac{1}{2}$

Spiritus Magnasomnigus

The human mind is, much like bendy spaghetti, an amazing thing. I have often read fascinating stories about people who, in times of great stress, recalled helpful information they never even realised they knew.

Take Tobias Treachery, for example, who found himself in a very stressful situation, if you call being stuck inside a cupboard with thousands of killer vampire bats feverishly trying to get in a stressful situation, which most people

would. In this highly stressful situation, Tobias recalled something he had once learnt from Mr Dungolly, a local scientist who was often invited to Huggabie Falls Primary School to give the children specialist science classes.

This was a great surprise to Tobias, because after years of attending the dreary specialist science classes of tubby old visiting scientist, Mr Dungolly, Tobias was pretty sure he hadn't learnt one single thing about science. He'd spent most classes daydreaming, sleeping, doodling drawings of penguins or passing secret notes to Cymphany and Kipp about which one of them could see the furthest up Mr Dungolly's expansive nostrils.

But as Tobias stared at some test tubes lying on the ground of the cupboard, he read a label: *Spiritus Magnasomnigus.* His mind raced back to a specialist science class from two years ago. He remembered Mr Dungolly standing in front of the class, reading from page 4017 of *The Bumper Book of Sciencey Stuff*, which he always lugged around with him: '*Spiritus Magnasomnigus* is an experimental chemical that scientists developed at the Huggabie Falls Centre for Extraordinary Chemicals and Substances.'

Two-thirds of the class were asleep at this point, and the other third was busy doing their English homework, but Mr Dungolly forged on. 'Derived from simple base elements, *Spiritus Magnasomnigus*'s uses are varied, however its primary purpose is as a powerful sedative. Contact with the epidermal layer—in other words, the skin—of experimental subjects has been known to render these subjects unconscious for up to twenty-four hours.'

Then Mr Dungolly had frowned at the dozing students. He was quite aware that he was considered to be the most boring expert to ever teach a specialist class at the school, even more boring that Ms Skeditt, the visiting watching-paint-dry expert. 'Although,' Mr Dungolly said, bitterly, 'I don't know why anyone bothers using *Spiritus Magnasomnigus*. Their experimental subjects could just attend my class. I'm sure it would be cheaper.'

It's amazing what the human mind can remember when it has to, and as Tobias stared at the test tubes he was amazed to remember Mr Dungolly's exact words about *Spiritus Magnasomnigus*.

Tobias knew that if any creature touched *Spiritus Magnasomnigus*, it would instantly fall asleep. Tobias's eyes continued to search the cupboard until his gaze fell on something equally useful. In the corner of the cupboard, leaning against the wall, were some back-mounted, pump-action poison sprayers. Tobias had seen the school gardener using these to kill weeds in the flowerbeds alongside the oval.

And then Tobias devised a plan.

'Quick,' he said, and he lunged for the test tubes and pulled out the stoppers on four of them, while Kipp and Cymphany looked on, confused. Tobias began to tip the fluid from the test tubes into the top of one of the back-mounted, pump-action poison sprayers. 'When the bats get in here, we need to spray them with this chemical,' Tobias explained. 'But whatever you do, don't let the chemicals touch your skin, or you'll fall asleep instantly.'

Kipp wanted to ask Tobias how he could possibly know that, because every time Mr Dungolly had talked about science, Tobias had been either asleep, doodling or passing notes to Cymphany. But this didn't seem like an appropriate time for asking questions—the bats were already clawing hundreds of tiny pinholes in the cupboard doors. So Kipp started helping Tobias pour the chemical into the sprayers. He trusted that his friend had a plan. Also, Kipp hadn't come up with a plan at all, other than just waiting and hoping that the bats would get bored after a while and go away.

As Cymphany was a baby hippopotamus, with hooves for hands and feet, she couldn't really help. '*Guurg*,' she said, which in hippopotamus language probably meant something like, whatever you are going to do, do it quickly because those killer bats are almost in here.

The holes in the doors were rapidly getting ripped wider and wider, and now hungry-vampire-bat noses were poking through. They sniffed their prey and their clawing got even more frantic. Their shrieking became so loud Tobias's ears started to ring.

'*Guurg, guurg, guurg*,' Cymphany screamed.

A bat finally squeezed its way into the cupboard and shot directly at Kipp, just as

Tobias hoisted the first pump-action sprayer full of *Spiritus Magnasomnigus* onto his back.

Tobias jerked the nozzle of the sprayer up and pumped a shot of *Spiritus Magnasomnigus* straight into the bat's face.

The bat was momentarily stunned.

'Good shot,' yelled Kipp.

'*Eu concordo, que tiro preciso*,' yelled Ralph, watching from the safety of his rat hole.

'*Burrg*,' yelled Cymphany.

But the bat was only momentarily stunned. To Tobias's horror it shrieked again, decided it wasn't going to get Kipp now, and streaked towards Tobias instead.

'Oh, dear,' said Kipp.

'*Oh, não*,' said Ralph.

'Bum,' said Tobias.

Cymphany didn't say anything. She hid her eyes behind her hooves.

Tobias squeezed his eyes shut and waited for the sharp bat talons and fangs to pierce his skin.

But nothing happened.

Tobias opened his eyes a peek, and to his surprise he saw the bat on the ground, fast asleep. It must have dropped mid-flight, just millimetres before it reached Tobias's face.

'It worked,' Kipp screamed.

Tobias smiled. 'Thank you, Mr Dungolly.'

No one else knew why Tobias was thanking Mr Dungolly, and they had no time to ask, because no sooner had the first bat fallen than twenty more ravenous bats had squeezed through the gap in the cupboard door, and now these bats were streaking towards Kipp, Tobias and Cymphany.

Strangely enough, Kipp and Tobias had been preparing for this moment all their lives, without even knowing it. They had both spent countless hours playing the video game *Super Outlaw Gunmen* at the Huggabie Falls Tenpin Bowling Alley. In this Wild West video game you used blue plastic guns to fire at hundreds of electronic outlaws on a video screen. The electronic outlaws charged towards you, getting faster and faster, and on the harder levels they ducked and weaved and tried to avoid your shots, and if you let too many reach the front of the screen the game was over.

Both Kipp and Tobias had spent so much money and time playing *Super Outlaw Gunmen* that they had managed to get right up to, and defeat, the final outlaw, Big Bad MacGruff, and his posse more than fifty times.

Ironically, Kipp's mother had often said that Kipp and Tobias were wasting their time playing that 'silly game' and should be spending their time doing something useful, like homework. But little did Kipp's mother know that the skills required to shoot electronic outlaws with plastic guns were remarkably similar to the skills required to shoot killer vampire bats with back-mounted, pump-action poison sprayers full of *Spiritus Magnasomnigus*. Skills which could now save their lives. If they had spent less time playing *Super Outlaw Gunmen*, like Kipp's mother wanted, and more time doing homework, then they would surely have been dead meat.

So next time your parents accuse you of spending too much time playing video games, you can refer them to this book and politely point out that there might be a time when you too are attacked by killer vampire bats, and the skills you learnt playing video games, which require you to shoot outlaws or fight an evil black knight or control a friendly, well-animated dragon, might just save your life.

Anyway, back to the story.

Feeling as though he was back in the video arcade, Tobias quickly blasted off three more pumps of his pump-action sprayer—*pump, pump, pump*—and felled three more bats—*thud, thud, thud.*

A quick commando roll under the other seventeen bats flying at him and—*pump, pump, pump, pump. Thud, thud, thud, thud.* Four more bats fell.

By now, Kipp had also got a pump-action sprayer full of *Spiritus Magnasomnigus* onto his back.

'I think there are more bats here than we've ever had outlaws in *Super Outlaw Gunmen*,' said Kipp, above the shrieking. 'But I think we've had enough practice at that game to make it out of this cupboard alive.'

Tobias grinned. 'Ready for stage two?'

Kipp nodded, and with five quick pumps of his sprayer he dropped five more bats.

Tobias raised his eyebrows. 'Not bad.'

Kipp shrugged cheekily. 'A bit rusty, but I'll get the hang of it.'

And so it continued: Kipp and Tobias pumped shots of *Spiritus Magnasomnigus* until the ground was littered with unconscious bat bodies. Cymphany stood between them, waving her hooves and trying to pull off some karate moves to ward off any bats that might be thinking of attacking her. But if you've ever seen a baby hippopotamus try to do karate, you'll understand why a baby hippopotamus has never become karate world champion, or even made into the top 7000.

Soon, with a combination of rolls, jumps, cartwheels and dives, and absolutely no help from Cymphany's hippo-karate, Kipp and Tobias fought their way out of the cupboard and down the hall. They were dropping about fifty bats a minute each, and those hundreds of dollars spent on *Super Outlaw Gunmen* were definitely proving a wise investment.

Cymphany's karate wasn't warding off the bats as much as she had hoped. When they swooped at her, she tried to scamper between the legs of Kipp or Tobias, and she roared when bats nipped at her tail.

As Kipp and Tobias felled more and more bats, some of the smarter killer bats, who didn't want to take an impromptu nap, began to flee.

'I think we're frightening them away,' Kipp cheered.

'Stage three,' said Tobias, pointing. 'The stairs.'

Kipp and Tobias ran down the corridor, trying not to trip over Cymphany as she clomped through their legs, dispatching bats with ease—*pump, thud, pump, thud*—until they reached the building's central stairwell, which led up to the third, fourth and fifth floors and down to the first and ground floors.

The whole building was suspiciously quiet. The only sounds were the squeaking of Kipp and Tobias's sneakers on the polished floors and the clomping of Cymphany's baby hippopotamus hooves.

'I don't like this,' said Tobias as he wheeled his pump-action nozzle around. 'Surely those bats haven't given up this easily.'

'It doesn't matter,' said Kipp. 'We have to get out of here. Who knows what else Mrs Turgan will send in when she discovers we've found a way to defeat her killer vampire bats.'

So the two children and the one baby hippopotamus made their way down the stairs, Kipp leading, Tobias at the back, and Cymphany in the middle, where it was nice and safe for an unarmed hippopotamus.

'Now that those bats are gone, I could really do with a lemonade,' Tobias said. 'We usually have a lemonade when we're playing *Super Outlaw Gunmen.*'

'Yeah, I'd love a lemonade too, said Kipp, smacking his lips together. 'I'm parched.'

They didn't notice that a certain baby hippopotamus at their feet was gawking at them incredulously, as if to say, oh, I'm *soooooo* sorry. You guys are a little thirsty. *Boo hoo.* Poor you. It could be worse. You could be a *BABY HIPPOPOTAMUS*!

They got past the first floor and were almost to the ground when there was a fluttering of wings from directly above.

Kipp looked up and gasped. The air was black with the flapping wings of a swarm of at least fifty killer vampire bats.

'Oh no,' said Kipp. 'Ambush.'

'That's not good,' screamed Tobias.

'*Urrrrggggaaa*,' said Cymphany.

Chaos errupted. Bats swooped down like a hailstorm—shrieking, flapping and clawing. A bat lashed across Kipp's face, knocking him over and sending his pump-action sprayer sprawling. Tobias dodged an attack, rolled onto his back and started firing wildly. He hit a few bats with *Spiritus Magnasomnigus*, but the rest swamped his sprayer, trying to yank it out of his hands.

It's interesting to note, at this point, that if you are ever stuck in a building with thousands of killer vampire bats hunting you that a stairwell is the perfect place for a swarm of bats to launch a surprise attack. Kipp, Tobias and Cymphany could be forgiven for not knowing this, as this was their first experience of a bat ambush. But if you're ever in this same situation, consider that a much safer option than stairs is a lift, as bats don't have fingers, so they can't push the button to open the door, and also bats never use lifts, as they absolutely despise elevator music.

Whoops, sorry. We are in the middle of quite an action-packed scene here, and I'm rambling on about lifts. My apologies. Where was I?

Oh, that's right.

Cymphany ducked swooping bats and tried to hide her head in her hooves. She roared as a bat sank its fangs into her tail.

'*Hurh, hurh*,' she said frantically, which meant something like, help, help, a bat has got me by the tail.

When Cymphany felt herself slowly hovering off the ground she thought, that's weird, I weigh too much for this to be happening. Surely a small bat can't lift a baby hippo?

Cymphany wheeled her hippo head around and what she saw made her hippo eyes open wide. It wasn't one bat lifting her, it was twenty. They'd grouped themselves together into a black, flapping mass, and were all lifting at once.

'*Huygh, huygh*,' Cymphany wailed, which, translated from hippo, meant, help, help, twenty bats are carrying me away by the tail. Hippos weren't meant to fly or we'd have been given wings. Help me, help me!

Tobias, who was in the middle of a tug-o-war with a swarm of bats over his pump-action sprayer, was the first to notice Cymphany was in trouble. He let the bats have his sprayer and he lunged, hurdling three steps and leaping with outstretched fingers. He just managed to catch Cymphany's front hooves.

Now that the twenty bats had to carry both a baby hippo and an almost-teenage boy, they started to struggle with the load.

'Hold on, Cymphany,' Tobias said. 'The bats can't carry both of us.'

'*Hurrug*,' Cymphany said, which was hippo for, great work Tobias. I'll be very happy to get my feet—I mean hooves—back on the ground.'

A group of nearby bats must have seen what was happening, because they stopped attacking Kipp and joined the bats trying to fly off with Cymphany and Tobias.

Just when Tobias, who was still hanging from Cymphany's front hooves, almost got his feet on the ground he noticed they were rising again. He looked up and saw that there were now more than forty bats clumping together to grip Cymphany's tail and they were lifting the two of them higher and higher.

'Man,' said Tobias. 'These killer vampire bats sure are smart.'

'*Hurrug*,' said Cymphany, which meant something like, now is not the time to be praising the bats' IQ, Tobias.

Meanwhile, Kipp, who had been retrieving his back-mounted, pump-action sprayer only to find out it had run out of *Spiritus Magnasomnigus*, scrambled over to try to help his friends. He was breathless and covered in bat scratches, but that didn't stop him from seeing the group of forty killer bats carrying Tobias and Cymphany up the middle of the big stairwell. He raced up the flights of stairs trying to catch up with them. They were up to the third level already, way too

high for either Tobias or Cymphany to jump down without hurting themselves. Kipp could see what the bats' plan was: to lift Tobias and Cymphany up really high, drop them and— Kipp gulped—*splat*.

Kipp had one chance to save his friends. He quickly thought of a plan. It was a very dangerous plan, but it was the only plan he had.

6

Mrs Turgan Sobs

The group of killer bats carried Cymphany and Tobias higher and higher, all the way up to the fifth level of the big stairwell. As they were going up, Tobias remembered there was a large window at the top of the stairwell, which he *really* hoped wasn't open.

As a wise person once said to me, hope can a very dangerous thing. True, he was trying to sell me life insurance at the time, but, still, he makes a good point. Tobias's desperate hope that the window wasn't open, made it even more crushingly devastating for him when he saw the window was open—and not just open a little bit but open so wide a hot air balloon could fit through it.

The bats carried Tobias and Cymphany, who were becoming more and more terrified by the second, out of the window, and before he knew it Tobias saw Huggabie Falls Primary School shrinking away beneath his dangling feet. Soon he could see the whole town of Huggabie Falls.

The only thing between Tobias and a very big fall—one that he probably wouldn't survive—were his hands clutching Cymphany's hooves, and the only thing keeping Cymphany up was the forty or so bats gripping her tail and flapping their wings madly.

Tobias tried to think of a way to escape this dangerous situation, but even if he still had his pump-action sprayer he couldn't use it on the bats now. The last thing he wanted was to put them to sleep—they were the only things preventing him and Cymphany falling from this alarming height.

Considering their current predicament, Tobias sort of wished they were back in the cupboard and he'd never remembered anything about *Spiritus Magnasomnigus*.

He looked up at Cymphany, who, as I might have already mentioned, was afraid of heights, and he saw she had her baby-hippo eyes clenched tightly shut.

'Don't worry, Cym, we'll be okay,' Tobias said, sure that he was lying.

'*Hurg*,' Cymphany squealed, which meant, I strongly suspect you are lying, Treachery.

Tobias was actually surprised at how brave he was being. He just hoped that Kipp was thinking of a way to save them right now, even though he was pretty sure that if Kipp was the one up here and it was him, Tobias, down there, he wouldn't have the first idea what to do.

A long way below him, Tobias could just make out an ant-sized Mrs Turgan, wearing a teeny ant-sized witch's hat, standing on the lawn in front of a matchbox-sized science building.

Even from this height, Tobias could hear Mrs Turgan screeching, 'Drop them, drop them.'

Unfortunately, the bats could hear her too, and Tobias and Cymphany found themselves experiencing the very unsettling sensation of falling towards the earth as fast as gravity could propel them.

The bats had let go.

So much for that ignorant bat keeper's claims that bats would never intentionally harm a human being. I hope he's reading this, and I hope he's feeling pretty darn silly right now, and taking note that not only will bats intentionally harm a human being, but they will also intentionally harm a baby hippopotamus. Although, even if he is, I bet Tobias and Cymphany are feeling worse.

Tobias saw the black swarm of bats getting smaller against the blue sky. He spun around and he saw the ground getting closer—much faster than he would have liked.

Oh dear, Tobias thought, we've been dropped.

Cymphany kept her hippo eyes tightly clenched shut. She knew they were falling, she knew they were high, and she didn't want to make things worse by seeing any of it.

Far below, Mrs Turgan rubbed her hands together with glee, as she watched the boy and the baby hippopotamus plummet. She wasn't sure where the other brat child was, but she knew he wouldn't be able to help his friends now, not unless he could get his hands on a ridiculously large trampoline.

And if you have any idea where Kipp might get his hands on such a thing, in the next ten seconds, then I really wish you would speak up right now, because things are getting pretty hairy for Tobias and Cymphany.

'I'm quite looking forward to my breakfast of child and hippopotamus pancake tomorrow,' Mrs Turgan cackled.

The child and the hippopotamus continued to plummet, getting closer and closer to the ground—spinning, flailing, helpless—and Mrs Turgan waited for that wonderful sound: a satisfying thud, signalling the child and the hippopotamus were history.

The thud came, but, strangely, it came from behind Mrs Turgan. She wheeled around, confused. She frowned. A minute ago, one of her key possessions had been lying on the ground. Now it was gone, replaced by an abandoned back-mounted, pump-action poison sprayer. But before she could wonder where it had come from an unexpected scream caught her attention.

'Good catch,' Tobias screamed.

'Thanks,' Kipp grinned, the wind rushing through his hair.

Tobias held on to Kipp with one arm and with his other arm he held on tight to Cymphany, because with her hooves she wasn't able to hold on tight herself. And they all needed to hold on very tight because they were travelling at a colossal speed, about one metre off the ground.

'I thought we were done for,' said Tobias.

'*Hurh*,' said Cymphany, which meant, thank you for saving us Kipp, but I think I'll just keep my eyes tightly closed if you don't mind, at least until I have got my hooves back on the ground.

'Our troubles aren't over yet,' said Kipp. 'I don't really know how to fly this thing.'

This thing Kipp didn't really know how to fly was Mrs Turgan's broomstick. He'd managed to manoeuvre it to catch Tobias and Cymphany, which was the important bit, and he'd quickly figured out the basic controls: you twisted the broom the way you wanted it to go and kicked its bristles to make it go faster. But now the broom was refusing directional twists, and it was bucking like a wild stallion, as if it had just realised it wasn't being flown by its master. But the worst part was that Kipp still hadn't worked the most important control.

'We're going very fast,' Tobias commented

as a tree whistled past within millimetres of his face. 'I'm almost afraid to ask—'

'No,' Kipp screamed in panic. 'The answer is no. I've got no idea how to stop this thing.'

Now, if you are ever caught on a runaway broomstick, and you're not able to brake, and you only have the choice of crashing into a shed full of farm animals or a shed full of fluffy pillows, then I would recommend the shed full of fluffy pillows every time. Unfortunately, Kipp, Tobias and Cymphany didn't have the option of a shed full of fluffy pillows, as they only had the shed full of farm animals in front of them.

This shed happened to be in the grounds of the Huggabie Falls Primary School, and was used for agriculture activities. Kipp, Tobias and Cymphany crashed through the wooden wall of the shed, cannoned through a yard containing some chickens, smashed through a pen, alarmed some pigs who were halfway through lunch, scared a goat so much it fainted and, finally, ended up face-first in the water trough of some rather startled horses.

But, thankfully, they had stopped, and, even more importantly, they were still alive.

Mrs Turgan's broomstick picked itself up, brushed itself off, spat bristles and flew off in a huff.

Kipp, Tobias and Cymphany pulled themselves out of the trough, gasping for breath and spluttering water, just as you would expect two children and a baby hippo who had come to an abrupt stop face-first into a horse trough would.

'Game over,' Tobias said cheerfully, wringing horse-trough water out of his shirt.

'Well played.' Kipp congratulated his friend. 'What an amazing plan those poison sprayers were. How you knew that chemical would put the bats to sleep, I'll never know.'

'I'll tell you about it one day,' Tobias said.

'It was pretty brave what you did.'

'Brave?' Tobias frowned. He was never brave. He didn't know what had come over him.

'But what about you?' Tobias said. 'Cymphany

and I were facing certain death until you risked your life to steal Mrs Turgan's broomstick.'

'It was nothing,' Kipp said modestly.

'*Hurrrrrrrrrg*,' said Cymphany, which meant, in hippopotamus, if you two are quite finished patting each other on the back, don't forget I'm still a baby hippopotamus, and now to top it all off this pig is looking at me like he wants a date.

Tobias looked around. 'Quick we'd better get out of here before Mrs Turgan—'

'Too late!' Mrs Turgan's voice echoed through the shed, alarming the children and the farm animals. She was standing in the two-children-one-baby-hippo-and-a-broomstick-shaped hole left in the side of the shed, and the broomstick was standing proudly beside her.

'Never send a bunch of dumb bats to do a witch's job,' Mrs Turgan hissed. 'I'll finish you children off myself, and, let me tell you, it will take a lot more than a splash of *Spiritus Magnasomnigus* to stop me.'

Kipp, Tobias and Cymphany sighed as one, as if to say, when is this crazy teacher going to give us a break?

Mrs Turgan began to fire off purple lightning bolts, which hit the shed's wooden walls, sending splinters hurtling through the air and farm animals diving for cover. The children and the baby hippopotamus ducked and crawled out of the shed through a back hatch, which, coincidentally, was exactly the right size and shape for a baby hippopotamus to fit through. They ran across the oval and back into the school.

Mrs Turgan took to the air on her broomstick, and soon her cackling laugh filled the air. 'I'm going to get you, you revolting kiddies.'

Kipp, Tobias and Cymphany ran around a corner and skidded to a stop. They found themselves staring at a high, solid brick wall.

'Oh no,' said Kipp. 'A dead end. Quick, let's go back.'

'I don't think so,' said Mrs Turgan, who had landed behind them, blocking their way back.

'*Gorbogh*,' Cymphany shouted, which in hippopotamus language meant, oh no, we're in big trouble.

'Oh no, we're in big trouble,' said Tobias, not realising that he'd repeated exactly what Cymphany had just said.

'Yes, you are!' said Mrs Turgan as she dismounted, and her mouth spread wide in an evil sneer. 'You are in very serious trouble, indeed, in fact I doubt you could be in any more trouble than you are right now. You've escaped me twice already, but, let me assure you, you will not escape a third time.'

'Mrs Turgan,' Tobias said urgently. 'We've been trying to investigate the extremely weird thing that happened.' He corrected himself. 'That is still happening. It's affecting almost everyone, and we need to stop it.'

'I don't care,' Mrs Turgan said, and her long warty nose twitched. 'You children skipped school, and the punishment for that is one zap of my wand for each of you.'

'What will that do?' Kipp asked.

'*Hugliff*,' Cymphany said, which meant, maybe it's best if we don't ask.

'Maybe it's best if we don't ask,' said Tobias.

'*Gurg*?' said Cymphany, which meant, I just said that.

Mrs Turgan grinned. 'It varies. Last week I zapped a boy I didn't like the look of and he became the size of a mouse. Unfortunately, soon after he accidentally found his way into one of my mouse traps, silly little thing.'

'You mean you kil...you kil...' Tobias was too petrified to speak properly.

'He was lucky,' Mrs Turgan said. 'There are far worse things that my wand can do, painful horrible things.'

'*Turg*,' said Cymphany, which probably meant, like what has happened to me.

'Yeah, like what has happened to Cymphany,' said Kipp.

'*Gurg*,' said Cymphany.

'Enough talking,' said Mrs Turgan. 'The

sooner I punish you, the sooner I can find some more disobedient children to punish.'

She held up her wand. 'Any last words?'

'Sorry guys,' said Kipp. 'I never should have suggested we skip school today. I got us into this mess.'

'*Hurg huuuurrrag*,' said Cymphany, which probably meant, don't be silly, Kipp—we all wanted to find out what was causing this extremely weird thing. You are a great friend who would never intentionally put us in harm's way.

'Don't be silly, Kipp,' said Tobias. 'We all wanted to find out what was causing this extremely weird thing. You are a great friend who would never intentionally put us in harm's way.'

'*Huppparg*,' screamed Cymphany, which meant, I'm really getting sick of everyone repeating what I say. When are you two going to learn to speak hippopotamus? You'd better learn quick, because we are probably only going to live for another two seconds.

'Say goodbye, kiddies,' said Mrs Turgan, as her wand hummed and sparked, and her broomstick clapped its bristles together.

Kipp, Tobias and Cymphany huddled together, hugging each other, and awaited their doom.

Mrs Turgan swished her wand.

It chugged and spluttered.

A frown spread across Mrs Turgan's face. She slapped the wand against the side of her robes, muttering, 'Silly thing. I just had it serviced last week.'

She tried again to zap the children, but nothing happened.

Kipp, Tobias and Cymphany couldn't do anything but huddle together and hope that nothing continued to happen.

After a few more tries, Mrs Turgan snapped her wand in half. 'Stupid twig,' she screeched. 'I never should have bought a second-hand wand in the first place.' She reached down and ripped a handful of blades of grass from a conveniently positioned tuft. 'You managed to deal with my bats, but let's see how you handle an army of deadly snakes,' she hissed at the huddling children and baby hippo.

She threw the blades of grass to the ground at the children's feet, and Tobias, Kipp and Cymphany leapt back in fear.

I'm guessing that the children and one baby hippopotamus didn't leap back in fear because they have a phobia of blades of grass, like a friend of mine, Atticus, has. Last I heard, Atticus had moved to Antarctica—one of the most blades-of-grass-free regions in the whole world. Unlike Atticus, I'm guessing Kipp, Tobias and Cymphany weren't scared of the actual blades of grass, but rather what the blades of grass might turn into, via Mrs Turgan's magic.

But the blades of grass stayed blades of grass, and they soon fluttered away in a light breeze.

Mrs Turgan looked at her hands as if they were a non-magical person's hands that had snuck onto her wrists when she wasn't looking. 'My powers,' she wept. 'They're gone.'

Then suddenly, in a flash of light, Cymphany stopped being a baby hippopotamus and turned back into a human girl.

'*Hurgug*,' she said. 'Oh, whoops, sorry, I'm still talking in hippopotamus. I meant to say, hooray, I'm not a baby hippopotamus anymore.'

Mrs Turgan gawked at Cymphany. And then her lip trembled, and she began to cry so much that she had to sit down.

It's weird how when you see someone crying, even someone who has been particularly horrible to you, you instantly feel sorry for them. The children looked at each other and then felt compelled to pat Mrs Turgan on the back.

'There, there,' said Cymphany, giving Mrs Turgan some tissues from her satchel. 'Don't cry, Mrs Turgan. Tobias, Kipp and I are going to find out what's causing all this normality and put a stop to it. You'll be back to your kid-zapping ways in no time.'

'Yeah,' said Tobias. 'It's nothing to worry about, just a temporary break in transmission.'

'Nothing to worry about?' Mrs Turgan sobbed, before blowing a big snotty mess into Cymphany's tissues. 'My powers are gone. How am I going to punish naughty children now?'

'Perhaps you could just start being nice to people,' Cymphany suggested.

'Nice?' Mrs Turgan blubbered.

'Yes, nice,' said Cymphany, as if to say, surely you must know what the word nice means.

And then Mrs Turgan began to cry even harder than before. 'Nice? I don't do nice!'

After a little while Mrs Turgan stopped crying, but then she realised that the only thing her broomstick was good for now was sweeping floors.

'I can't fly anymore,' she wailed. 'I'll have to catch public transport. That's a fate worse than death.'

'Honestly,' Kipp sighed. 'Can't you just walk

until we get this weirdness sorted out.'

'Walk?' Mrs Turgan frowned.

'Yes, walk.'

So, after another bout of crying, Mrs Turgan did just that. She trudged off slowly, dragging her now-ordinary broomstick behind her.

Kipp, Tobias and Cymphany stood and watched her go. It must have been a strange feeling for them to see a woman who used to be petrifying now not very petrifying at all.

I know how the children felt—exactly the same thing happened to me, with my fear of keyboards. This was an affliction that greatly hampered my career as a writer. But after years of hypnotherapy, I am no longer petrified of keyboards, and I'm now able to use one, albeit only while blindfolded.

Half an hour later the children found themselves on the corner of Digmont Drive and Digmont Drive.

'Well, we didn't learn too much today, did we,' Cymphany said in a strangely upbeat voice, despite the day's traumatic events. 'We'll have to meet up tomorrow and continue our investigations. But not too early. I like to sleep in on Saturdays.'

Cymphany waved goodbye to Kipp and Tobias as she walked up the street to her house.

When she was almost there, she turned and shouted, 'Oh, and by the way, in case you wanted to know, the capital of Argentina is Buenos Aires.' She grinned. 'Just thought you'd like to know.'

As Tobias and Kipp walked along Digmont Drive, Tobias said, 'What is it with Cymphany and capital cities lately?'

Kipp shrugged. 'I was thinking the same thing myself. She's acting weird, which is weird because she used to be the only normal person in this town.'

They walked for a bit without saying anything, until Tobias said, 'Why are you so upset about your family turning normal?' Isn't it—'

'What I always wanted?' Kipp looked thoughtful. 'Yeah, I guess. But it doesn't feel right. Something bad is happening to Huggabie Falls and we have to stop it.'

'Although,' Tobias said, 'Mrs Turgan turning normal today did save our lives and stop Cymphany from spending the rest of her life as a baby hippopotamus.'

'That's true. Imagine being a baby hippopotamus forever,' said Kipp.

They continued along Digmont Drive, turned up Digmont Drive, then crossed over Digmont Drive to Kipp's house.

Jam

Kipp, Tobias and Cymphany weren't able to meet each other the next day. Kipp's parents had organised a family barbecue at the park, which was a very normal way for a normal family to spend a Saturday. Kipp tried pretending he was sick so he wouldn't have to go, but his mother said, 'Oh dear, perhaps we'd better take you to see Doctor Tillgang.'

Now, I'm sure you'll agree that some children have a fear of going to the doctor. I myself would rather be smeared in mashed banana and lowered into a cage full of hungry gorillas than visit my local doctor. But if you are a child living in Huggabie Falls and you are scared of going to the doctor, it is with very good reason. Huggabie Falls' doctor, Doctor Terrence Tillgang, was not just a doctor, he was also a werewolf. As long as you didn't visit him when there was a full moon you were generally okay, but it was always a good idea to keep your pockets full of silver bullets just in case. And even if it wasn't a full moon you were still likely to leave Doctor Tillgang's surgery covered in bite marks and, if he happens to be moulting, wolf hair.

So, even though Kipp desperately wanted to investigate the extremely weird thing that had happened, he didn't want to go see Doctor Tillgang even more, so he was forced to make an immediate recovery from his fake illness.

Kipp tried to ring Tobias all morning, but the phone at the Treachery house was engaged, which wasn't unusual—the Treachery family so often had people ringing them requesting they repay their debts that Tobias's mum would regularly take the phone off the hook. Strangely, Kipp couldn't reach Cymphany by phone either, and Kipp couldn't reach Tobias or Cymphany on Sunday either. Which I, as storyteller, agree is quite odd. Not as odd as mismatched socks, but odd nonetheless.

On Sunday, Kipp's parents took him tenpin bowling. At the bowling alley Kipp wasn't even tempted to play *Super Outlaw Gunmen*— he was too preoccupied thinking about the extremely weird thing that had happened, and his extremely normal family.

Afterwards the Kindle family went to see the movie *The Pirate King* at the Huggabie Falls cinemaplex. As Kipp lined up at the candy bar to pay for his popcorn he saw Mr Haurik in a neighbouring line, holding a chocolate bar and a giant cola. Mr Haurik no longer had his wooden leg—he now had a new artificial limb that looked just like a normal leg—and he was without his parrot and his eye patch and, strangest of all, he was wearing a suit. Kipp left his line and went over to Mr Haurik's line.

'Mr Haurik?' said Kipp, as if to say, Mr Haurik, is that really you?

Mr Haurik looked down. 'Hello there, Kipp. Fancy meeting you here. Are you going to see *The Pirate King*? I've heard it's an excellent movie.'

'But, Mr Haurik, you hate pirates! Why would you be going to see a movie about them?'

'Hate pirates?' Mr Haurik didn't seem to understand. 'It's funny you should say that, because just this morning, as I was looking at myself in the mirror, I realised that the way I was dressed was a bit ridiculous—in fact, I looked a bit like a pirate myself.'

'I see,' said Kipp. 'And you just noticed that this morning?'

'I also sold my caravan,' Mr Haurik announced.

'Sold your caravan!' Kipp yelped, as if to say,

but we love that caravan—it's what makes you Mr Haurik.

'Yes, well, it was a bit outrageous, wasn't it? A bit...what's the word?'

Kipp sighed. 'Weird?'

'Yes, weird.' Mr Haurik smiled. 'And I don't want to be weird, do I? I think I'm going to buy a nice normal house and become an accountant, which unfortunately means you children won't be able to visit me anymore, as I'll be too busy calculating people's taxes, wearing suits and doing whatever else it is that accountants do.'

'Excuse me, youngster, do you want to pay for your popcorn?' said a cinema attendant. Kipp realised they had got to the front of Mr Haurik's line.

'No, thank you,' said Kipp. 'I think I've lost my appetite.'

Kipp didn't sleep at all that night, and the next morning he was an hour early for school. He was quite annoyed when Tobias and Cymphany arrived.

'Hello, at last,' Kipp said sharply. 'I've been trying to get in touch with you all weekend. What happened to you guys? You'll never believe what happened to Mr Haurik.' And Kipp told them all about his encounter with Mr Haurik at the cinemaplex.

Cymphany apologised for being unreachable over the weekend. 'My days were jam-packed,' she explained.

When someone uses the expression their days were 'jam-packed', they are usually referring to the fact that their days were very busy. But as Cymphany explained to Tobias and Kipp, when she used the expression jam-packed she was actually referring to the fact that her days were packed with jam. She had woken up on Saturday morning to find her living room full to the ceiling with boxes, all of them filled with jars of jam. Her dad was unpacking them and smiling broadly. 'I've started a great new job at the jam factory,' he announced. 'One bonus is we get all the free jam we like. So I've brought home a hundred boxes.'

'So,' Cymphany said. 'For breakfast I had jam on my porridge, followed by jam on toast. For lunch we had a jam pie, followed by scones with jam and cream. And for dinner we had chicken with jam sauce and then for dessert we just had jam—we ate it straight out of the jar with spoons. Dad started wondering what we should do with all the leftover jam containers. So he built us a new letterbox out of them. He thought it looked cool.' Cymphany rolled her eyes.

'Then Dad was saying he could build other stuff out of the empty jam jars. He has already built a kennel for Patches and a new fence at the front of our house, and he has started building us a second carport. He reckons just another hundred boxes of jam and it will be all finished.'

'Yum,' said Tobias. 'You're lucky. I love jam.'

Cymphany glared at him. 'We've become known on our street as those weird jam people.

And, well, jam is okay for a treat, but I am so sick of jam, now. I made sure that I got out of the house early this morning because Dad said he was making a jam omelette. *Blegh*!' Cymphany stuck out her tongue and screwed up her face to show how much the thought of jam omelettes disgusted her, in case the word *blegh* had not been convincing enough.

'Well,' said Tobias. 'That's nothing. Wait until you hear about my weekend. On Saturday, my parents won the lottery, and my father paid off all his debts, so we no longer have debt collectors knocking on our door all day and night. My parents have pulled all the boards off our windows and our house looks totally normal now. And, for the first time ever, my sister and I could play in the backyard without having to worry about the neighbours throwing rotten fruit at us. We had a big party on Saturday night, and all our neighbours came over. Now, people like my parents so much that they're telling my father he should run for mayor of Huggabie Falls. Have you ever heard anything so bizarre? My father, the most disliked man in all of Huggabie Falls, and now they want him to be the mayor!'

Kipp shrugged his shoulders. 'Same for me, I'm afraid. We went to the park yesterday. My parents watched television. My father helped me with my homework. All completely normal stuff. It was horrible.'

'The strange thing is,' Cymphany said, 'I was always envious of you guys, with your weird families. You don't know what it's like being a girl from the only normal family in town. That's why I started all the capital-city stuff—I wanted to make myself more weird.'

Kipp smiled. 'I'm glad you had a reason—we just thought you'd gone crazy.'

Tobias nodded. 'Completely potty.'

'But,' Cymphany continued, 'now that my family is finally weird, and I've got everything I always wanted, I just want them to be normal again. I don't want to be known as that weird jam girl forever. I just wanted a little bit of weirdness. I mean, my dad is talking about filling all our mattresses with jam. He kept talking about how soft it would be to sleep on.' She put her hands on her hips. 'I am *not* sleeping on a jam mattress.'

Kipp nodded. 'Well, let's consider what we know so far. We know that Mr Dark is hiding something. He could even be behind all this extremely weird stuff that is happening.'

Tobias and Cymphany agreed, so they

decided that after school they would hide outside Felonious Dark's office again, as they had done on Friday when the previously magical Mrs Turgan had caught them and attempted to kill them with bloodthirsty vampire bats.

For the rest of the school day there was no chance whatsoever that Kipp, Tobias and Cymphany would concentrate on any schoolwork. On Monday mornings Mrs Turgan usually taught them geography, followed by English and then mathematics, or she spent the morning zapping children with her wand, whichever took her fancy. But instead, Mrs Turgan spent the whole morning curled up in the corner, sobbing.

Ug Ugg was usually more than happy to take over when Mrs Turgan didn't want to do any teaching, or when she was too busy transforming a child into a cumquat, but Ug Ugg was absent, which was astonishing, because Ug Ugg hadn't missed a day of school in five years. So the children had to teach themselves, which, to their credit, they mostly did.

Cymphany usually enjoyed the geography part of Monday mornings, because she worked hard memorising capital cities, but today her mind was far away, thinking about horrible jam, and how nice it had been when she was normal.

And Tobias quite liked Monday-morning English, usually, but he too spent the whole morning, as his mum would say, 'off with the fairies'. Funny thing was, he was quite happy about the new situation—his parents weren't treacherous anymore and the inside of his house was bathed in sunlight.

In the time when they would usually be doing maths, Kipp fell asleep. He was tired because he hadn't slept much all weekend. He wouldn't usually have dared do this if Mrs Turgan was her normal self, because Mrs Turgan loved turning napping children into pillows.

Eventually, the children left a bawling, thumb-sucking Mrs Turgan and went to physical education class, where Henrietta Humpling told Kipp, Tobias and Cymphany she was actually not one-third werewolf and one-third vampire anymore. 'I am now just Dutch,' she explained.

'How is that possible?' Tobias asked from behind the pommel horse, where he was hiding from Coach Peltin Pilkon, who was in the process of forcing children to do rope climbs.

'Yeah,' said Kipp. 'A person's race can't just change.'

'Well,' said Henrietta. 'It appears as though there was a mix up on my birth certificate, and my grandfather on my mother's side was not a vampire, and my grandmother on my father's side was not a werewolf. It turns out everyone was just Dutch, so now I'm just entirely Dutch.'

'And how do you feel about that?' asked Cymphany.

'Well, it's pretty good, I suppose. At least I can now have a normal breakfast, instead of having cornflakes with a glass of blood.'

'*Yeeeck*,' said Tobias, with a similar

expression on his face to Cymphany's *blegh* face from earlier.

'I know.' Henrietta nodded. 'Disgusting, isn't it. I never really liked cornflakes either.'

Two Little Sailboats
and a School of Vegetarian Piranhas

'Chin,' said Tobias.

'Cornea,' said Cymphany.

'Calf muscle,' said Kipp

'Ummm...' said Tobias, thinking hard for a moment. 'Chin bone.'

'Protest,' shouted Cymphany, with a triumphant smile on her face. 'Chin and chin bone are not two separate answers.'

'They are so,' said Tobias.

'Are not.'

'The chin is the whole chin area, and the chin bone is one part of the chin.'

'As if!' Cymphany laughed. She was using her satchel as a pillow as she lay on her back on the grass. 'You're treacherous, Treachery.'

'Well, then.' Tobias opened his mouth and pointed inside. 'My answer is cavity.'

'Cavity!' Cymphany sat up. 'Cavity is not a part of the body.'

'It's a part of my body,' Tobias said. 'The dentist said it will be till I stop eating so many Fizz Blast lollipops.'

Kipp, Tobias and Cymphany were playing their favourite waiting game, the name-a-part-of-the-body-that-starts-with-the-letter game. It was a great game for passing the time because you could easily spend a whole hour debating whether bum crack and bum crevice were two separate answers or the same thing, and time was something Kipp, Tobias and Cymphany had plenty of. They'd been hiding across the road from Felonious Dark's office all afternoon.

'Anything yet?' Tobias asked Kipp, whose turn it was to keep watch to see if anyone left Felonious Dark's office, especially if it was Felonious Dark himself.

Attention readers: I should warn you, at this point, that this is one of the longer chapters in the book. You might be thinking, so what, just let me get on with it will you? It's only getting longer the more you jabber on about it. But I just thought I'd give you warning in case you were thinking to yourself, I'll just finish this chapter before I go and get myself a drink, or before I go to the toilet. It might be best you go to the toilet now, and get yourself a drink and maybe even make yourself a sandwich, because having three regular meals a day is very important, and then you will be nice and relaxed and able to enjoy this chapter fully, because everyone always enjoys things more with an empty bladder and a stomach full of delicious peanut-butter-and-salt-and-vinegar-potato-chip sandwich. So if I were you I'd go right now, and I'll put extra spaces in so you have plenty of time to get back and don't miss anything.

All done? Good. Now, where was I? Had I got to the bit where Tobias said, 'Anything yet?'

Oh yes, that's right, I had.

'No,' said Kipp. 'Mr Dark's receptionist has been out for thirty coffee breaks in the last hour, but apart from that, nothing.'

Now you, as an astute reader, have probably already worked out we're not here to read about the children doing the letters C to Z in the name-a-part-of-the-body-that-starts-with-the-letter game, and you would be correct, because seconds later Felonious Dark did emerge from his office building.

'Wait a second,' said Kipp. 'Forget what I just said. It's Mr Dark.'

Kipp, Tobias and Cymphany scrambled to their knees and crawled together behind a bush, aware they hadn't been all that well-hidden spread out lying all over the grass.

Felonious Dark stood in front of his office, extended his long thin neck to look up and down Digmont Drive, and mumbled something to himself before skulking off down the road.

Cymphany adjusted her glasses and bit her lip. 'I guess we'd better follow him,' she said.

'We need to keep our distance,' Kipp said. 'We don't want Mr Dark seeing us. He doesn't seem like a very nice man.'

I have to note, at this point, that Kipp saying Felonious Dark didn't 'seem like a very nice man', goes down in history as one the biggest understatements ever uttered by anyone— perhaps second only to when Huggabie Falls resident Mr Jackson Jolley pulled back the

curtain and peeked outside during the great blizzard of eighty-seven, and said to his wife, 'I'd better get my coat. It looks a tad nippy outside.'

Legend has it that if you peer deep into the iceberg that still roams the surface of the bottomless lake, you can see a glimpse of Jackson Jolley's frozen form in the middle, with a boy-is-my-face-red expression on it.

Tobias must have thought Kipp's comment was sort of obvious too, because he nodded as if to say, you can say that again.

So Kipp, Tobias and Cymphany followed Felonious Dark down Digmont Drive, where he turned left and went up Digmont Drive, then crossed over Digmont Drive and made his way down Digmont Drive.

'Did you ever wonder,' said Tobias as they hid behind a street lamp, 'who the idiot was who decided to name every street in Huggabie Falls Digmont Drive? It's incredibly confusing.'

'I often wonder why a lot of things in Huggabie

Falls are the way they are,' said Cymphany, as they ducked behind a picket fence. 'I don't think any other town is so full of weirdness.'

After they'd spent all that time and effort keeping their distance and hiding from Felonious Dark, Kipp, Tobias and Cymphany bundled around a corner and almost ran straight into his back. Only Kipp's quick thinking saved them as he lunged and pushed Tobias and Cymphany behind a red parked car.

Felonious Dark was chatting to a man in white overalls who was standing on a ladder painting a street sign. As Kipp, Cymphany and Tobias tumbled to the ground behind the parked car, Kipp held his finger to his mouth—the international signal for *shush*.

Cymphany pointed, Kipp and Tobias nodded and the three of them crawled on their stomachs under the car until they were centimetres away from Felonious Dark's feet. Felonious Dark's pants were too short, exposing his white ankles and grubby socks. Cymphany held her nose and scrunched up her face, because the smell wafting from Felonious Dark's feet was very unpleasant. Tobias and Kipp's faces looked similarly disgusted, but at least they could all now hear what Felonious Dark was saying to the man painting the street sign.

'Are you changing the name of the street?' Felonious Dark asked.

They heard another voice, which must have been the painter's, say, 'Yeah. The local council passed a new bylaw this morning. Now streets can be called names other than Digmont Drive.'

'Really? That's surprising,' Felonious Dark said, and even though Kipp, Tobias and Cymphany couldn't see his face they could tell he was smirking.

'Not really,' the painter laughed. 'We should've done it years ago. It really is flipping confusing. I mean, can you imagine trying to deliver mail in this town? No wonder the last thirty Huggabie Falls posties have gone insane.'

Tobias raised his eyebrows and glanced at

Kipp and Cymphany, as if to say, weren't we just talking about this?

'So, what is this street going to be called now?' Felonious Dark asked.

'Tim Street,' the painter said. 'Because that's my name, Tim. And the street is being named in honour of me, because I'm the one with the paintbrush.'

Felonious Dark chuckled. 'I suppose that's fair enough,' he said. 'Keep up the good work, my man.'

Felonious Dark said his goodbyes to the painter and was on his way.

Kipp, Tobias and Cymphany waited till Felonious Dark was halfway down the road before crawling out from under the car. Tim the painter was a big man with a bushy red beard. He seemed a little surprised to see three children crawl from under a car, but he smiled anyway. 'Hi, kids. Nice day for a walk down Tim Street.'

He had finished painting the street sign *Tim Street* in big black letters. He took off his cap and wiped his forehead with it as he stepped back and admired his work.

'This weirdness is—' Cymphany stopped. 'Wait a minute, I mean, this *normalness* is spreading at an alarming rate.'

Kipp nodded. 'We have to find out what Mr Dark has to do with all this.'

Kipp, Tobias and Cymphany said goodbye to Tim, and continued following Felonious Dark. Eventually they all ended up one kilometre out of town at the misty lake, which was called Misty Lake.

Misty Lake was so named because it was: a) a lake, and b) always covered by a thick blanket of mist. If you ever go for a boat ride on Misty Lake you'll find you won't be able to see more than three metres in front of you, which is useless information, as boat rides on Misty Lake are strictly prohibited, since the lake is the source of all of Huggabie Falls' drinking water.

Considering this fact, Kipp, Tobias and Cymphany found it odd that tied to a small jetty grinning Tobias. 'Hilarious, Treachery. And good plan, Kipp. We can use the bucket to bail water out. Now, we'd better hurry, you can't see very far on Misty Lake and Mr Dark has already got a big head start on us.'

Kipp, Tobias and Cymphany climbed into half-full-of-water boat, which sat even lower the water once it contained three children. water level inside the boat immediately ed to rise, but Cymphany was able to keep wn with swift bailing. Neither Kipp, Tobias ymphany knew how to sail, but there were ars, so Kipp and Tobias rowed the boat ross the Misty Lake while Cymphany e little red bucket to bail water out as fast ould.

a while, the water level in the boat o at least be staying the same, maybe ng down a bit, but soon Cymphany 'I think we're sinking. I don't get it— g was working, but now, no matter bail, the water inside the boat is still

at the edge of the lake were two little wooden sailboats. Actually, come to think of it, why did a lake where boats rides are prohibited have a jetty in the first place?

Kipp, Tobias and Cymphany sat crouched behind some bushes. They were further surprised to see Felonious Dark climb into one of the little sailboats, untie it from the jetty and sail off into the mist.

While we are on the subject of nonsensical things, a boat *sailing* into the mist seems like a contradiction to me. Because the word mist implies still, non-windy air. If there was any wind, say the sort of wind required to 'sail' a sailboat, then it would surely blow all the mist away, and the lake would henceforth be called Windy Lake. So, I'm not exactly sure how Felonious Dark managed to sail his sailboat away into the mist, but, as I've said before, I'm just a storyteller, and I have no control over these things. Perhaps this is just one of the many,

many, many weird things about Huggabie Falls that cannot be explained, or maybe Felonious Dark had a little, completely silent and undetectable motor attached to the back of his boat—whatever the reason, we haven't got time to find out right now.

'I suppose we'd better follow him,' said Kipp.

'Not across Misty Lake,' Tobias said, shuddering. 'What about the piranhas?'

Now, if you know anything about dangerous marine life, then you will know piranhas are carnivorous freshwater fish with very sharp teeth. They're usually only found in waterways of the Amazon rainforest, but it so happened that Misty Lake was also full of them.

'Don't worry about them,' said Cymphany. 'They're vegetarian.'

'Vegetarian?' Tobias said. 'Really?'

'My father told me,' Cymphany said, as though that confirmed it, even though her father was not a marine biologist, or even a fisherman,

and therefore nowhere near being an e these things.

'I've heard that too,' said Kipp. ' Lake piranhas are the world's only piranhas.'

Tobias thought about this for don't know why I'm surprised. Th Falls, after all,' he said.

So Kipp, Tobias and Cymp to the second sailboat, only in very good shape for sailin fact, it wasn't in good shape bathtub: it was full of holes

'Well, this is no good,' thing is more submarine

'Wait a moment,' something shiny and r edge of the lake. 'W bucket?'

'Don't be silly, K all fit in that little r

Cymphany rai

the
in
The
start
it do
nor C
two
out a
used th
as she
For
seemed
even goi
frowned.
my bailin
how fast I

rising, and the edge of the boat is still sinking.'

'I'll bail; you row,' said Kipp to Cymphany, as if to say, perhaps I can bail a bit quicker than you can, which is obviously what we need.

A few minutes later, the situation was still not improving. Tobias took a turn at bailing and put every ounce of effort he had into it, but the boat's rim was getting closer and closer to the water.

'This is hopeless,' said Tobias as he looked around. 'I can't see Mr Dark anywhere, and we're almost sunk.'

'You're right,' said Cymphany. 'I think the shore is back that way.' She pointed into the mist. 'If we row and bail hard, we might be able to make it back without having to swim.'

'Wait,' said Kipp. 'Can you hear that?'

As people often do when the phrase 'can you hear that?' is used, Tobias and Cymphany stopped talking and listened. There was a faint thrashing and splashing noise. The children began to scan the water.

'There!' Cymphany pointed.

Kipp and Tobias followed the line of Cymphany's point and saw in the distance a cluster of about a hundred thrashing objects in the water, which was moving rapidly towards the boat.

'I think that's a school of piranhas?' said Tobias. 'The way they're feverishly thrashing around reminds me a little too much of Mrs Turgan's killer vampire bats,' he said, as if to say, I hope you were right about that whole only-vegetarian-piranhas-in-the-world business, Kipp.

'They do seem to have a hungry look about them, don't they,' said Kipp, as if to say, I hope I was right about that whole only-vegetarian-piranhas-in-the-world business, Tobias.

'I'm sure there's nothing to worry about,' said Cymphany, frowning. 'They're definitely vegetarian. But I do wonder why are they coming towards us? Does anyone have a stick of celery in their pocket?'

Tobias and Kipp both gave her strange looks, as if to say, we are not even going to bother checking our pockets for celery, because we are schoolboys, and the odds of finding celery in any schoolboy's pocket are pretty low.

'Well, they must be after something,' said Cymphany.

The school of thrashing piranhas was getting very close now.

'I just thought of something,' said Kipp grimly. 'You know how everything in this town is becoming normal all of a sudden?'

'Yes,' said Cymphany, keeping one nervous eye on the approaching fish.

'Well, suppose the piranhas have turned normal as well.' Kipp looked as if he didn't really want to finish his sentence. 'Which would mean they are—'

'Not vegetarian anymore,' Tobias said, as he turned white.

The rim of the boat's hull dipped underwater at that point, so all three children did the only thing they could do: they climbed the boat's little mast, which was the only bit still above water.

Kipp and Cymphany went up first, and just as Kipp reached down to help Tobias, a piranha launched from the water, hungrily snapping its teeth.

There was a loud crunch, and Tobias froze.

'*Arrrrrrrr,*' he screamed. 'My bum!'

'What happened?' Cymphany said, as she scrambled to keep a good hold on the mast. 'Did you get bitten?'

While Kipp held onto him, Tobias quickly checked his backside. 'I'm okay,' he said with a huge sigh of relief. 'But the little fishy beast bit off my pocket, and right through my undies too, I think. I can feel fresh air on my behind!'

Cymphany laughed, although it wasn't really a funny situation. 'That was a close one,' she said, stating the extremely obvious.

They looked down and saw the piranha, with Tobias' pocket and part of his undies in its mouth. Other chomping piranhas converged on

the fabric, until it was completely shredded and half digested.

'Oh dear,' said Tobias. 'If they did that to a little bit of pocket and undies fabric, imagine what they'll do to *us*.'

The boat's tiny mast could barely support the weight of the three children clinging to it, and it groaned ominously in the breeze—even though we've already established that the presence of breeze on Misty Lake is impossible, but somebody please tell the breeze that, because it was there anyway.

The frantic piranhas surrounded the base of the mast. The rest of the boat was at least thirty centimetres underwater now. So to anyone passing it would have appeared as though three children were out on Misty Lake riding a pogo stick.

'This is a very bad situation,' said Kipp, who had obviously been to the same stating-the-extremely-obvious school as Cymphany. 'We're still sinking.'

'And we've got no *Spiritus Magnasomnigus* to save us this time,' added Cymphany, dismally.

'Can anyone see anything?' Tobias said, and he looked around madly.

But there seemed to be nothing around them except mist, water and piranhas.

'What about your satchel, Cym?' Kipp asked, clambering to keep high on the mast. 'Is there anything in there that can help us?'

Cymphany shook her head grimly. 'I'm afraid not. Only more of those chocolate-chip cookies we had the other day, and they won't be any good to us now.'

Tobias gulped. He was actually a tad peckish, but he could hardly enjoy chocolate-chip cookies from Cymphany's satchel at a time like this. Or at least, not enjoy them very much.

'Well, this may be it,' Cymphany sighed, as if to say, it might be time to say our final goodbyes, before we become piranha food. 'We may have escaped Mrs Turgan, but I don't know what can save us this time.'

'There's only one thing to try,' said Tobias.

'What's that?' Kipp asked, hoping his friend had a brilliant escape plan.

'Well,' said Tobias nervously. 'I could jump in and swim for it. The piranhas are bound to chase me. If I don't make it back to land at least the two of you might be able to.'

'But,' said Kipp. 'Then you'll—'

'I know,' said Tobias, trying to act braver than he felt. 'But if it will help you two get away it's a sacrifice I am willing to make—you are my best and only friends in the whole world, after all.'

Kipp and Cymphany were in awe of their wonderful, caring friend, who, despite his Treachery family name, was so loyal he would sacrifice his life for the chance to save theirs.

'We can't let you do that,' said Cymphany. 'Either all of us make it out of this or none of us. *Ahhhhhh.*' Cymphany flinched as a flying piranha shot past her face and a sharp tooth flicked the end of her nose.

'We haven't got time to argue,' Tobias said. 'In a few seconds this mast will be underwater. There is no other way out of this.'

With that Tobias leant back and started to release his grip on the mast.

'No,' Kipp shouted. 'No, Tobias.'

Cymphany also screamed for her brave friend to stop.

Now, as storyteller, I feel I have to interrupt at this point to reassure you that Tobias didn't jump. But I honestly believe he would have, if not for the fact that a voice rang through the air just in the nick of time.

'I wouldn't do that if I were you,' bellowed a smiling Felonious Dark, as he and his sailboat emerged from the mist. 'The piranhas will have you shredded and eaten in seconds, and then your friends as well. None of you will make it anywhere near the shore.'

'Help us,' yelled Cymphany.

Felonious Dark laughed a wheezy laugh.

'Help you? Why would I do that?' The thin cruel man casually steered his boat in close to the children, but not close enough for them to jump on board. 'I was the one who put the holes in your boat.'

'You are evil,' Cymphany screamed.

Felonious Dark laughed again. 'Of course I am. I never claimed to be otherwise.'

Kipp, Tobias and Cymphany sank lower and lower. They were only half a metre above the water now. Felonious Dark was taking great pleasure in watching as they screamed and dodged the flying, teeth-gnashing piranhas.

Just when Kipp, Tobias and Cymphany thought Felonious Dark was going to sit by and watch them perish, he pulled in closer and yanked the children, one by one, into his boat.

Kipp, Tobias and Cymphany huddled together at one end of Felonious Dark's boat, shivering and shaken by their ordeal.

Felonious Dark watched the mast of the sinking sailboat finally disappear under the water. 'You've lost my red bucket,' he said in a bemused tone. 'I expect compensation for that.'

'Your red bucket?' Kipp asked, as if to say, that's odd because I found that red bucket half-buried in the sand.

'Well, of course.' Felonious Dark smirked. 'The red bucket I partially buried for you to find. I knew you'd think you could bail the water out fast enough, but I also knew eventually you'd be overcome and then you'd have no chance of making it back to shore.'

'You mean you had this all planned?' Tobias asked in disbelief.

Felonious Dark seemed especially proud of himself. 'It was a beautifully devious plan, wasn't it. And it would have worked. Only, I realised that if children's bones started turning up in the Huggabie Falls drinking water a few too many questions might be asked. It was almost as good as my plan last week to ring Mrs Turgan and tell her I'd seen a few truant children loitering outside my office.'

'You fiend,' yelled Cymphany, which is exactly what I would have yelled if I'd been there.

The realisation came over Kipp, Tobias and Cymphany that they'd been tricked by this evil man not once, but twice, and they all felt exceptionally gullible.

'What are you going to do with us?' Tobias asked.

'That's enough questions for now,' Felonious Dark hissed. 'You children should just be happy to be alive. Now, sit back and enjoy the ride.'

9

A Lesson in Genetics

Actually, Felonious Dark's suggestion that Kipp, Tobias and Cymphany sit back and enjoy the ride reminds me of another Huggabie Falls resident who enjoyed rides. I think now might be a good time to tell you about him.

Pidge Priestly loved roller-coasters. At the age of nine he went on his first amusement-park roller-coaster ride. He liked it so much he went on it again, and again, and again—thirty-four times in a row. The only reason he stopped was because the amusement park closed for the evening.

At ten the next morning, an amusement-park worker found Pidge waiting outside for the amusement park to open, so he could ride the roller-coaster again.

Pidge's parents soon became quite concerned with their son's obsession. Pidge even said he would live on a roller-coaster if he could.

Then, many years later, he read an article in the paper that said Huggabie Falls was the only town in the world where it was legal to build your house on a roller-coaster. So Pidge moved to Huggabie Falls and built his house on a roller-coaster.

Pidge loved it, but he soon discovered that it's quite expensive to keep a house on a roller-coaster running twenty-four hours a day, so he was forced to sell rides on his house. People could pay to sit in his lounge room, his dining room, or even in his little vegetable garden, while enjoying a roller-coaster ride. They often asked Pidge how

he could enjoy living on a constantly moving and dipping, and sometimes upside-down house. Pidge would just shrug and say he liked to sit back and enjoy the ride, and the only downside was he couldn't flip pancakes anymore.

So I hope you enjoyed the story of Pidge Priestly and how he came to live in Huggabie Falls. Kipp, Tobias and Cymphany had heard of Pidge Priestly, and, just like me, they'd thought of him when Felonious Dark said sit back and enjoy the ride. The children doubted that even Pidge Priestly, who enjoyed rides more than anyone, could enjoy this ride. When you go on a normal ride you usually do it of your own free will, not out of being kidnapped, and you are not normally surrounded by hungry not-vegetarian piranhas.

So, subsequently, the children did not sit back and enjoy the ride. Instead, they continued to huddle together, shivering from the cold and keeping a close eye on Felonious Dark.

Felonious Dark stood at the other end of the boat, steering it with one oar, and looking like an evil gondolier sculling a gondola in Venice. He whistled happily to himself and started to sing a song. Felonious Dark was not a good singer. The song went:

Normal, normal, normal.
I like things that are normal.
They are better than things that are weird.
Everyone agrees with me,
even that guy with the beard.
Normal, normal, normal.

Felonious Dark pointed at Kipp, Tobias and Cymphany. 'Sing along, children. You know the words.'

Normal, normal, normal,
Normal, normal, normal,
Normal, normal, normal.

Kipp, Tobias and Cymphany did know the words, or really just the one word repeated many times, but they didn't sing along because the song wasn't that good, and even if it was good they wouldn't have felt like singing. They were cold and scared, and Felonious Dark's smelly feet were making them all feel nauseous.

Felonious Dark kept singing, and steering, all the way to the gigantic Huggabie Falls water plant, which sat on an island in the middle of

Misty Lake. This water plant was responsible for pumping water from the lake, filtering it, and piping it into the town for the residents of Huggabie Falls to drink, and shower in and flush toilets with. The plant was full of rusty pipes and vats of freshly filtered water.

Felonious Dark steered the boat through one of the grand brick-archway entrances and he, Kipp, Tobias and Cymphany drifted into a cavernous domed room that had a vast metal platform on one side. A creepy woman with white hair, glasses and a long white lab coat—the sort scientists wear—stood waiting on the platform. Nearby, two big muscly men in suits sat at a little foldaway table playing cards. They didn't look like scientists—they looked more like henchmen.

Felonious Dark steered the boat over to the edge of the platform. He sprang onto the platform and tied the boat to a bollard with a thick rope.

'What's this?' the creepy scientist said to Felonious Dark.

The two big muscly henchmen looked up for a moment, but they must have decided Kipp, Tobias and Cymphany weren't that interesting, because they were soon taking turns throwing cards down on the table again, and every few seconds one of them would slam a hand down and shout, 'Snap!'

'These kids were snooping around,' Felonious Dark said, responding to the creepy scientist's question. 'This one is Kipp Kindle.'

The creepy scientist looked at Kipp, and her eyebrows shot up. 'Oh, so you're Kipp Kindle,' she said.

'That's right, I am,' Kipp said, defensively. He was used to people knowing who he was, due to his famously weird family, and it wasn't usually in a good way. 'Who are you?'

The creepy scientist laughed. 'You used to have the weirdest family in Huggabie Falls. You're our biggest success story.'

'Success story?' Cymphany humphed and crossed her arms.

'And this is Cymphany Chan,' Felonious Dark explained.

'That means you must be Tobias Treachery,' the creepy scientist said, studying Tobias.

Tobias glanced down at the water, as if he was considering whether he might be better off in with the piranhas.

The creepy scientist smiled at Tobias's apprehension. 'You must be enjoying the fact that your family is no longer the most disliked family in Huggabie Falls.'

Kipp, Tobias and Cymphany had no idea what to say next. They were all a bit shaken— which was not surprising considering they had almost been eaten by piranhas only a short while ago, and now they'd been kidnapped and brought to an isolated water plant, and had no idea what this creepy scientist or the evil Felonious Dark, or those two muscly henchmen had planned for them. So silence seemed like the best option at that point.

'Well, come on then.' The creepy scientist

gestured at the platform. 'Get out of that boat. We're not going to hurt you.'

Felonious Dark grinned evilly at them, as if to say, well, maybe these others won't hurt you, but I wouldn't be so sure about me.

'Why should we trust you?' Kipp asked the creepy scientist. 'You've obviously had something to do with the extremely weird thing that has happened, and because of Mr Dark we came very close to being eaten by piranhas.'

The creepy scientist glared at Felonious Dark. 'Felonious, we're supposed to be doing a good thing here, not hurting children.'

Felonious Dark shrugged. 'What? I'm evil. That's why you hired me.'

The creepy scientist eventually convinced the suspicious children to get out of the boat—she even ordered one of the muscly henchmen to get Kipp, Tobias and Cymphany some fizzy drinks from some other room.

While one muscly henchman was gone the

other muscly henchman rearranged all the cards in the deck, giggling mischievously.

When Kipp, Tobias and Cymphany were given their fizzy drinks, they were sensible enough not to drink them. They had all been warned not to accept gifts from strangers. 'Especially,' Kipp's mother had once said, 'drinks from creepy scientists or their henchmen.' Which was very wise and, now that I think about it, suspiciously accurate advice. When the creepy scientist asked why they didn't want the drinks, Tobias said, 'We don't trust you. These drinks could contain anything.'

I suspect the drinks were orange flavoured, as in a recent survey of creepy scientists across the nation, it was found that nine out of ten creepy scientists prefer orange flavoured drinks. But I do think it was wise for the children not to accept the strange drinks, especially if they weren't aware of the survey.

The creepy scientist laughed. 'You are very smart. Perhaps I should tell you what we are doing here. That might put your minds at ease.'

Kipp, Tobias and Cymphany all looked at each other. They most certainly did want to find out what was going on here, which was why they'd followed Felonious Dark in the first place.

The creepy scientist continued. 'I'm a scientist who works for the government, and a few years ago I identified the weird gene.'

'The *weird* gene?' Tobias said, frowning.

'Yes,' the creepy scientist said. 'Do you know what genes are?'

'Of course,' Cymphany said. 'Genes are the little coded bits of us that determine what colour hair we have, how tall we are going to be and all that stuff.'

'We've got a smart one here,' said the creepy scientist and she winked at Felonious Dark. 'Genes make up your DNA. All human beings are made up of DNA...'

The creepy scientist then started explaining DNA to Kipp, Tobias and Cymphany, but I won't write about that. Explanations of DNA are about as exciting as watching paint dry. When someone uses the expression 'as exciting as watching paint dry', they are referring to the fact that watching paint dry is the most boring thing imaginable, because it takes hours and hours for paint to dry, and you can't actually see anything happening, so all you are really doing is spending hours and hours sitting, staring at a painted wall. But, still, Kipp, Tobias and Cymphany would have preferred that to spending hours and hours listening to the creepy scientist explain DNA.

And if I were to write down everything that the creepy scientist said you'd soon put this book down and go look for that painted wall to sit in front of.

So I'll just cut to the chase, which is another expression. It means get to the point, and get to the point is another expression which means hurry up and get on with the story, which is what I bet you want me to do, so I will.

✴

'So,' Cymphany said, relieved that the creepy scientist had *finally* finished explaining DNA. 'Now that you've spent three hours telling us all about DNA, can you tell us what a *weird* gene is, which was our original question?'

The creepy scientist smiled. 'Well, a few years ago the government put together a list of one thousand normal genes. For instance, people who have a gene that says they are going to have blond hair, that's a normal gene, a gene that says you are going to be short-sighted, or one hundred and eighty centimetres tall, or have green eyes—all normal genes. And then the government put together a list of one thousand weird genes. For instance, if you have a gene which says you are going to have X-ray vision, or be one thousand four hundred and nineteen centimetres tall, or have checked pink and yellow skin—those genes were all declared weird genes.'

Kipp crossed his arms. 'How does having a list of weird genes help anyone?'

'I'm glad you asked,' said the creepy scientist

and she smiled. 'Once we were able to identify all the weird genes, we were able to identify people who were likely to become weird, and that meant we could control the spread of weirdness within normal society.'

'I don't get it,' said Tobias. He looked like someone had just given him a particularly difficult mathematical equation to solve.

'I think I do.' Cymphany had an angry look on her face.

The creepy scientist seemed amused. 'Do you really, little girl?'

'Yes, I do.' Cymphany turned to Tobias and Kipp. 'Haven't you always wondered why everyone and everything in Huggabie Falls is weird? And how all these weird people and weird things ended up in the same place?'

'Coincidence?' Tobias suggested, convincing no one, least of all himself.

'No. Don't you see? The government has arranged all this.' You could tell from the tone in her voice that Cymphany was furious. 'It's like when my parents first decided to move to Huggabie Falls. It was because my dad got this transfer at his work, a big promotion. I remember him saying that he didn't even realise his work had a branch in Huggabie Falls.' She scowled at the creepy scientist. 'I bet that's because they didn't. It was the government, wasn't it? Forcing my dad's company to get rid of him, setting up the new job here, buying us the new house, and a new car. How could Dad refuse?' She clenched her teeth. 'And why? All because he had a slight lean.'

The creepy scientist grinned. 'You're an exceptionally smart girl, Ms Chan. I must admit your father was only a little bit weird, nowhere near as weird as some of the other people we've sent to Huggabie Falls. But he had one of the thousand identified weird genes, so he had to be relocated here.'

Kipp thought about his family and how weird they used to be. He missed their weirdness.

The creepy scientist continued. 'You see,

normal people just don't like weirdness around them. The average person can't handle sitting next to a real live witch on a bus, and parents don't want their kids going to a school where some of the students are vampires. Weirdness freaks people out! So, many years ago the government began identifying all the children born with weird genes, and monitoring them, and when those people started displaying weirdnesses the government decided to gather them all together in one place, and that's how Huggabie Falls began.'

Kipp, Tobias and Cymphany were silent for a few moments, the way people often are when they've just been flooded with unsettling information.

'That's terrible,' Kipp said at last.

'Is it?' The creepy scientist chuckled. 'No one is forced to come to Huggabie Falls, everyone comes of their own free will.' She turned to Cymphany. 'Like you said, Ms Chan, your father had a job offer too good to refuse.'

One by one Kipp, Tobias and Cymphany realised that what the creepy scientist had told them was true. Their families had all come to Huggabie Falls voluntarily, and, furthermore, they were free to leave anytime they liked. But despite the fact they had all had been tricked into moving here, they now loved Huggabie Falls and couldn't imagine living anywhere else.

'But the one thing I don't understand,' said Tobias, 'is why all of a sudden everyone in town is turning normal. How is this possible if we are all supposed to have these weird genes?'

'I'm glad you asked that, Mr Treachery,' said the creepy scientist. 'After many years of study, and lots of experimentation, my colleagues and I have managed to develop'—the creepy scientist leaned in close as if she was about to tell the children an exciting secret—'a cure for weird genes.'

'A cure?' Kipp, Tobias and Cymphany said in unison. Then Kipp added, 'you can't cure *genes*.'

The creepy scientist waggled her finger.

'Correction. You never *used* to be able to cure genes. But we've developed a weirdness cure, which attacks and eradicates weird genes. For the last few months our employee Felonious Dark has been feeding the weirdness cure into the Huggabie Falls water supply. In another twenty-four hours everyone in Huggabie Falls will have consumed a full dose and the weirdness cure will be irreversible.'

'Irreversible!' Kipp gulped. 'You mean, my parents will never be weird again?'

'Wait, wait,' Cymphany shouted, waving her hands. 'But my parents are becoming more weird, not less weird.'

Felonious Dark snorted. 'Whoops.'

The creepy scientist winced. 'Yes, a slight miscalculation there. I don't think we should ever have classified your father's 'slight lean' gene as one of the thousand weird genes. Unfortunately the weirdness cure has had the opposite effect on your father's genes.'

Cymphany gasped. 'You mean in twenty-four

hours everyone in this town will be normal, and my family will be the jam family—forever?'

The creepy scientist put her hands up. 'Like Felonious said, whoops.'

Right then, Cymphany was about to explode, but it was at this point that both she and Kipp noticed that Tobias was deep in thought.

'Tobias?' Kipp nudged his friend. 'Are you okay? Aren't you as outraged about this weirdness cure as we are?'

'I guess.' Tobias shrugged. 'But with all the sunlight in our house my vitamin D deficiency is better, and our neighbours love us now, and we can get a decent night's sleep without debt collectors banging on the door all night.'

Cymphany's face dropped. 'Oh, Tobias, I'm so sorry. Here we were only thinking about ourselves. I never stopped to think that you might actually want this to happen.'

The creepy scientist was nodding. 'You see, getting rid of weirdness in the world is good for everyone. Kipp, you'll be happy your parents are normal, once you get used to it.'

'I guess,' Kipp said, but he also frowned, as if to say, I don't think I will at all.

'And Cymphany,' the creepy scientist continued. 'Who cares if your family is going to keep eating lots of jam? Jam is yummy. Surely it's better than being in the most disliked family in Huggabie Falls. Do you really want your friend to go back to that?'

Cymphany sighed. 'No.'

'So why don't you children run along then, and just enjoy being normal, except for Cymphany, of course. Again, really sorry about that, Ms Chan.'

Felonious Dark nodded. 'Come on, let me escort you back to town.'

So Kipp, Tobias and Cymphany climbed back into Felonious Dark's boat and began the long journey back across Misty Lake. And they all agreed that perhaps this cure for weirdness really was the best thing.

But it didn't feel like the best thing. The only

person without a glum look on his face was Felonious Dark. He whistled merrily and sang a few more rounds of the normal song.

They sailed passed the tip of the stranded mast of their old sunken boat, and before long they were back on the Misty Lake jetty.

'You kids have a nice normal day, now.' Felonious Dark put extra emphasis on the word normal. Then he laughed and sailed away, disappearing back into the mist.

'So,' Cymphany said once they were alone. 'After all that work to find out what was causing the extremely weird thing, now that we've found out, we don't even want to stop it.'

'And we were almost killed numerous times,' Kipp added.

'I'm really sorry,' said Tobias. 'I feel terrible.'

'Don't feel terrible,' Kipp said. 'It's great that your family is no longer treacherous, and I'm sure I will get used to my new normal family.'

'And jam is yummy,' said Cymphany, in a very non-committal tone.

After a few moments of uncomfortable silence, Tobias said. 'I guess we'll all see each other at school tomorrow.'

'Righto,' said Cymphany.

'Sure thing,' said Kipp.

And the children walked off in separate directions to their homes.

The end.

Okay, sorry about that. A bit of a storyteller's joke there, I'm afraid. That's not really the end. Some of you readers might have thought it was and that Cymphany was doomed to be known as the jam girl forever, and that Kipp would never again have his weird family back, and that they would both make this sacrifice for their friend Tobias, so he wouldn't have to live in a treacherous boarded-up house anymore.

But if you thought that, then you couldn't be more wrong. Actually, you could be more wrong. For instance, if you thought this book was a small European mountain range, well, that would be more wrong.

But there is more to this story. You still have to learn why Kipp's family is the weirdest in all of Huggabie Falls. I've been keeping that a secret. And we can't possibly let the creepy scientist win so easily. So we'd better get on with the story and find out what really happens. After you've grabbed yourself another peanut-butter-and-salt-and-vinegar-potato-chip sandwich, that is. I wish you could grab one for me, too. But I can't stop for a sandwich because you need to know what happens next.

Okay, if you've got yourself another sandwich now, then I'm jealous, but let's move onto chapter ten and another account of another one of Huggabie Falls' weirdest occupants—Ferris Farmelade.

A Peach, an Italian Painter and Three Letters

All his life Ferris Farmelade had eaten nothing but French fries. They were the first thing he ate as a baby, and ever since he had never wanted anything else.

Ferris's parents weren't too happy with this arrangement. But if they tried to feed Ferris something else, he would clamp his little baby mouth shut so hard you couldn't prise it open with a crowbar.

Ferris's parents eventually gave in and

started feeding Ferris nothing but French fries, with a variety of dipping sauces, despite doctors' warnings that Ferris would be unlikely to survive past his first birthday.

Defying medical predictions, Ferris did live past his first birthday. True, by the time he was five Ferris had already had two triple heart bypasses, but he was still alive.

By the age of eighteen Ferris had astounded doctors everywhere by still being alive. At a worldwide health summit, Ferris's case was discussed and experts theorised that Ferris had eaten so many thousands of tonnes of French fries that his body had actually learnt, inexplicably, how to get all the nutrients it needed from only one food source.

When a twenty-four-hour MegaBurgerWorld that served mega-tubs of French fries opened in Huggabie Falls and offered Ferris a job as chief French fries sampler, Ferris moved to town. And he had lived ever since in a house next door to MegaBurgerWorld, which was, coincidentally, also next door to the Treachery family home.

So, for the past fifteen years Ferris Farmelade had lived next door to the Treacherys and had eaten nothing but MegaBurgerWorld French fries. And not only were the huge amounts of deep fried potatoes he consumed not killing him, but he actually seemed to be in perfect health.

Okay, so now I've finished telling you the tale of Ferris Farmelade, another one of Huggabie Falls' weirdest occupants, we can get back on with our story. You might be wondering why I even told you Ferris's story. Well, it's because, on the day that Tobias, Kipp and Cymphany met the creepy scientist who told them about the weird gene cure, Ferris Farmelade was coming home from his shift at MegaBurgerWorld. As ususal, Ferris had a mega-tub of French fries under his arm and a bucket of sweet chilli sauce to wash them down with.

Halfway down his driveway Ferris stopped suddenly. He stared at a small something sitting in the middle of his driveway.

It was a peach.

Now this was not unusual, in and of itself, as there was a peach tree on the corner of the opposite property, and peaches quite often rolled across the road and onto Ferris's driveway. But what was unusual was that Ferris had a feeling he'd never felt before.

Ferris felt like eating the peach.

He felt like picking it up, taking a bite, and seeing what it tasted like. It was the first time Ferris had ever wanted to put anything in his mouth that wasn't a French fry.

But now, for reasons he didn't understand, but you probably do, he couldn't get one thought out of his head. The thought was, I wonder if that peach is even better than French fries? So Ferris put down his mega-tub, picked up the peach, rolled it over in his hands for a few seconds, and took a bite into its juicy flesh.

Tobias Treachery arrived home half an hour later, having just said goodbye to Kipp and Cymphany on the corner of Digmont Drive.

Tobias couldn't help but notice there were two ambulances parked in Ferris's driveway and a crowd of people on Ferris's front lawn.

'What's going on?' Tobias asked Mateo Mazzine, who lived down the road. Mateo was an Italian painter, which in his case meant he regularly threw paint on unsuspecting Italians.

'That silly fool Farmelade ate a piece of fruit,' said Mateo. 'He's eaten nothing but French fries for the last forty years and today, for no apparent reason, he decided to try a piece of fruit.'

'Really?' said Tobias. 'Shouldn't that be a good thing?'

'You would think so,' said Mateo. 'But the paramedics reckon that after forty years Ferris's body has evolved into a fat-fuelled machine. Whereas most people shouldn't eat too much fat, Ferris's body now can't survive without it. And the sudden impact of eating fruit caused his whole body to go into shock.'

'Is he going to be okay?' Tobias asked.

'Hard to say. They're rushing him to hospital now.' Mateo shook his head. 'I just don't understand what possessed Ferris to try a piece of fruit after all these years?'

But Tobias knew exactly what had possessed Ferris or, to be more accurate, what had cured him of his weirdness. It was the weirdness cure that everyone in Huggabie Falls was consuming every time they drank from the town's water taps.

'What about you, Mateo?' Tobias asked. 'How's your painting going?'

Mateo shrugged. 'To tell you the truth, this morning for the first time ever I decided I would paint on canvas. I painted a picture of a horse. And I really enjoyed it. I think I might paint on canvas all the time from now on. Actually'— Mateo scratched his head—'I don't know why I ever started throwing paint on Italian people in the first place. It really is a bit silly, and the Italians I throw paint on do tend to get quite annoyed.'

Mateo shook his head and chuckled. 'Isn't that incredible? The day Ferris decides to eat a piece of fruit is the same day I decide I don't want to paint Italians anymore? What are the odds of that?'

'Yes, what an incredible coincidence,' Tobias said, deadpan.

Tobias left Mateo and began walking up his own driveway. The Treachery home used to be the darkest and dingiest house on the street, all boarded up, with rotten fruit all over the lawn, and, as if even the sky disliked the Treachery family, there always seemed to be gloomy clouds hovering above.

But now the sun shone down on the Treachery house, which was actually a quaint cottage, and the birds chirped in the blue sky above. All the rotten fruit was gone and there were fresh daisies in the garden beds. The white picket fence along the front had been repaired and the letterbox, which used to be crammed full of final-payment notices, had an apple pie sitting on it with a note that said it was from Beryl Bott from number eleven 'for the Treachery family to enjoy'.

Tobias smiled. The weirdness cure seemed like a very good thing for him, and it was about time something good happened to Tobias.

He knew Kipp didn't like his new normal family, but he'd probably get used to it, and he might even grow to like it. And Cymphany? Well hadn't she always wanted a weird family? Now she finally had one, so who was she to start complaining? And jam *was* yummy. And Ferris Farmelade? It was unfortunate that he was on his way to hospital, but maybe his body would get used to eating fruit now, which had to be a good thing. And Mateo? Well, at least the Italian people in Huggabie Falls no longer had to live in fear of getting drenched in paint.

All in all, Tobias thought, this town might be better off without weirdness.

He couldn't wait to get inside and see what his new, normal family was up to. Perhaps his father would be throwing another mayoral-campaign party, and inviting the whole street. Or, even better, maybe the Treacherys would just have a nice family dinner together.

But, as it turned out, none of these things were happening inside the Treachery house, because no one was home. The house was silent, and there were three notes on the dining-room table.

Tobias read the first note. It was written on pink perfumed paper, which was the paper Tobias's sister always used. It read:

Tob,

Tell Mum and Dad I won't be home tonight. Since our family has become so popular I've been invited to loads of parties and made lots of new friends. I'm staying at Rachel's tonight, Becca's tomorrow night, and on Wednesday night I'll probably be at Penelope's house. Who knows what I'll be doing after that, but with so many friends I hardly have enough days of the week to stay over at all their houses or enough hours in the day to go shopping with them all. Isn't it wonderful!

Ta for now,

Tish.

After reading the note, Tobias sighed. It would be strange not having Tish around as much anymore. She was a best friend to Tobias as much as she was his sister.

But it was nice for her that she was so popular now. Tobias read the second note. It was written on 'Mayoral Candidate Theodore Treachery' letterhead paper. It read:

MAYORAL CANDIDATE THEODORE TREACHERY

Tobias, my boy,
Can't talk. Gotta run. Many things to sort out with all this mayoral stuff. Very, very, very, very, very, very, very busy. In fact no time to even write this note. Won't be home for tea tonight, tomorrow night, the next night—actually I'll just have my assistant call and let you know the next time I will be home for tea. You never know with all this mayoral stuff.

Regards,
Your father
(soon to be Mayor of Huggabie Falls).

Tobias frowned. If his dad became mayor of Huggabie Falls then he would probably be even more busy and spend even less time at home.

Tobias felt unsettled. With a shaky hand, he picked up the third note. It had been scribbled so quickly it took him a while to decipher it. It read:

Dear Tobias,

Sorry, won't be home for tea tonight. There should be something in the freezer you can defrost. I've become so popular—I've joined the golf club, the tennis club, the Huggabie Falls horse riders' association, and the list goes on and on. Your father and I are filming his new television commercial for his mayoral campaign tomorrow. If Mrs Bott drops around with another apple pie, make sure to put it in the fridge. I doubt I'll get a chance to eat any of it as I'm super busy going to functions, but if you see her make sure to say thank you, it was delicious, and I can't wait to attend her cooking class next Sunday.

Hugs and kisses,

Mum.

After reading the final note Tobias had to sit down. The whole family seemed very happy about their new popularity, but Tobias wondered what the point of being popular was if it meant you never got to see your family? Before the weirdness cure, the Treachery family had spent every night together. Tobias, his parents and his sister would play board games until the late hours, and talk for hours and hours about all sorts of things. Even though they were disliked by everyone else in town, the members of the Treachery family adored each other.

Tobias sat alone, slumped on the couch, for three hours. The house was silent except for the slow methodical tick of the grandfather clock in the hallway.

Finally, Tobias said out loud, 'Stuff this,' and he raced into the kitchen.

11

Three Minutes

Most people use watches to keep track of time. Huggabie Falls resident Webber Warbleton used egg timers. Every single activity Webber did during his day, he timed with three-minute egg timers. He used one egg timer to time brushing his teeth, one for having a shower, one for getting dressed, one for eating breakfast, one for feeding his dog, Floppy, and two for playing fetch with Floppy, because Floppy loved to play fetch. He used five egg timers consecutively to time his fifteen-minute drive to work, then one-hundred-and-sixty three-minute egg timers to time his eight-hour workday, and at night he carefully laid out, in toppling domino fashion, one-hundred-and-forty-seven three-minute egg timers to time his sleep, with the final egg timer positioned to fall onto his forehead and wake him up in the morning. In total, Webber owned four-hundred-and-eighty three-minute egg timers, the precise number required to time each twenty-four-hour day perfectly.

Now, I know what you're probably thinking. Why would someone want to time their whole day with three-minute egg timers? Or, to be more accurate, why would someone want to map out their whole day with four-hundred-and-eighty three-minute egg timers?

For Webber Warbleton, it all started about ten years ago. Back then, Webber was an extremely disorganised person who was always late for work, and Webber's boss told him that if he was late for work one more time he would be sacked.

Unfortunately, Webber slept in the next day, and by the time he woke up he realised he had only three minutes to get to work. This was not possible as it usually took Webber fifteen minutes just to drive to work. But Webber loved his job and didn't want to get the sack, so he decided he simply had to make it to work in three minutes.

As Webber bolted through his apartment, pulling on his work pants, he saw a three-minute egg timer on the kitchen bench, and he had an idea. He flipped the egg timer over. He knew if he could get to work before the trickling sand emptied from the top of the timer to the bottom, he would keep his job.

To Webber's surprise, under the immense pressure of the egg timer, he made it. Admittedly, he did have to drive through a number of people's backyards and up a big ramp to leap over a row of nine buses in the process. But he made it.

It didn't take Webber long to realise that with the pressure of egg-timer timing he was able to do things much faster than he ever had before.

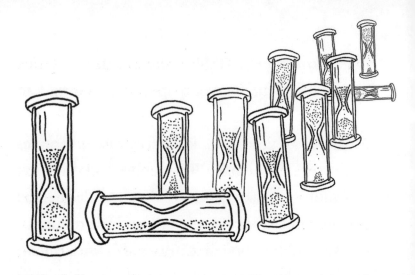

So Webber started carrying egg timers with him everywhere he went, to see what else he could do in three egg-timer minutes.

Soon Webber could do all his grocery shopping in three minutes; he learnt how to read a book in three minutes; bake a four-tiered wedding cake in three minutes; run three kilometres in three minutes; and, most impressively, he learnt how to assemble a small garden shed, complete with concrete flooring, in three minutes, which included the time it took him to drive to the hardware store to buy a measuring tape.

Webber Warbleton soon came to believe

that anything could be accomplished in three minutes, and he had yet to be proven wrong.

It usually took Tobias Treachery ten minutes to walk from his house to Kipp's. But today Tobias was in a very big hurry. A little while ago he had been happy his family was no longer treacherous. But now he realised that treachery was keeping his family together.

So, as he left the house, Tobias grabbed a three-minute egg timer from the kitchen bench. Today Tobias was going to test out Webber Warbleton's theory that you could do anything in three minutes if you tried hard enough.

Once he was outside, Tobias flipped the egg timer and ran for it. He jumped fences, ran through lounge rooms, even trampolined over a trampoline shop, and, amazingly, he made it to Kipp's house just as the egg timer ran out.

'Thank you, Mr Warbleton,' Tobias said to himself as he ran down Kipp's driveway.

Tobias went round to Kipp's bedroom

window and tapped on it with the egg timer—
Rap tap tap.

A sleepy-faced Kipp opened his window.

'Tobias, what is it? Why have you got an egg timer?' Kipp asked, as I'm sure you would too if one of your friends tapped on your bedroom window, in the middle of the night, with an egg timer—unless impromptu, late-night egg-cooking is something you and your friends do.

'Never mind that right now,' Tobias said, as he climbed through the window. 'C'mon, get ready.'

Kipp rubbed his eyes. 'Ready for what?'

'We have to get Cymphany. We have to stop this extremely weird thing that is happening.'

'But'—Kipp was confused—'what about your family?'

'But, nothing. My family was fine just the way they were. Sure, we were treacherous, but at least we loved each other and spent time together.'

Kipp was still confused, but he wasn't about to ask too many questions. He was just thrilled to hear that Tobias wanted to stop the extremely weird thing that was happening. It had been another night of horrific normality in the Kindle household. That evening they'd played charades, which was just ridiculous.

'So,' Kipp said as he got his big warm coat out of his wardrobe and put it on over his pyjamas. 'Are we going to get Cymphany right now? In the middle of the night?'

'I think we have to,' said Tobias, 'from what the creepy scientist told us, by tomorrow morning the effects of the weirdness cure will be permanent.'

'Yes,' said Kipp, 'I'll just sneak into Dad's workshop and grab a torch.'

At this point in the story, it concerns me that readers will be under the impression that I, as storyteller, am condoning the actions of Kipp and Tobias, and soon also Cymphany. I know I've talked about their misdemeanours before, but the fact of the matter is that so far in this story Kipp, Tobias and Cymphany have done so many things wrong that the only way I can effectively detail them is by using a numbered list. They are as follows:

1. They have skipped school.
2. They've entered strange and potentially unsafe buildings.
3. They've talked to strangers.
4. Kipp lifted a heavy aquatic mammal without properly bending his knees.
5. They've handled dangerous chemicals without reading the safety instructions and wearing appropriate safety clothing.
6. They've sprayed those dangerous chemicals on animals, and therefore could be charged with animal cruelty.
7. They've disobeyed the command of a teacher, which is wrong even when that command is, 'Stop, so I can zap you with my wand.'
8. They've jaywalked, albeit while on the run from that same murderous teacher.

9. They didn't ensure they were wearing lifejackets before boarding a boat, which was particularly reckless considering they'd already discovered the boat was full of holes.

There is probably other stuff that I've forgotten, but the point I want to make clear is that I do not condone or encourage any of these actions, and I must point out (again) that I am merely a storyteller, relaying, but not controlling, an adventure. I can just see the letters from parents now:

```
Dear Mr Cece,
My child attempted to lift a water
buffalo last week and severely hurt
his back in the process. When I asked
him where he got the idea that a
young child could lift a heavy aquatic
mammal, he directed me to your book.
As such, I blame you for my son's
injuries and enclose a large bill for
his medical expenses.
You should be ashamed of yourself.

Signed,
Disgruntled mother.
```

Even though I've just finished listing the various wrong doings of Kipp, Tobias and Cymphany, I now have to write about many other improper activities they were involved in.

Kipp and Tobias snuck out of their homes in the middle of the night, collected Cymphany, and then all three children broke into Felonious Dark's office.

Now, while the children felt they had to break their curfews, and indeed the law, to stop the extremely weird thing that was happening in Huggabie Falls, it does not excuse what they did, and I urge readers not to follow their example.

There is an expression that says 'Crime doesn't pay', and this expression suggests that if you commit a crime you won't benefit from it. Of course, this expression is about the silliest expression ever, because most of time the only reason people commit crimes in the first place is to benefit from them. Technically, the expression should be 'Crime *does* pay, but you shouldn't do it because it is *wrong*'.

Kipp, Tobias and Cymphany committed a crime by breaking into Felonious Dark's office and searching through his rusty filing cabinets. And in doing so, they found something that most certainly benefited them. They found blueprints—in other words maps of the layout—of the Huggabie Falls water plant.

Kipp unfurled the largest blueprint and held it up. Cymphany shined the torch on it, and they huddled together to study it.

'Look,' said Tobias, pointing. 'This note here says that the weirdness cure is being stored in these big red canisters.'

'And,' said Cymphany pointing to another spot on the blueprint, 'the canisters are being loaded into this vat, here, which feeds straight into the water pipes for Huggabie Falls.'

'So'—Kipp couldn't point to anything because he was already using both hands to hold up the big blueprint—'if we can get our hands on those canisters and get rid of the weirdness cure, then we can save the town?'

Kipp, Tobias and Cymphany smiled at each other.

'Wow, that was easy,' said Cymphany.

Then Tobias's smile turned into a frown. 'Yes, it was, wasn't it—a little bit *too* easy.'

While we are on the subject of expressions, I've just thought of another one. It was probably the same expression Tobias was thinking of when he said a little bit *too* easy. Have you ever heard of the expression, 'The calm before the storm'? It was originally an expression sailors used to describe the period of still air, and calm water, and lack of birds in the sky, that comes before a storm.

Smart sailors know that the birds have all nicked off and found shelter because they know a big bad storm is on its way, and the air is still because the wind gods are inhaling, and the water is calm because it's conserving its energy to thrash twenty-metre high waves over the top of any boats stupid enough to be in its path.

Nowadays, the expression is not only used by sailors at sea, but also by anyone experiencing an eerie period of calm that could be a premonition of chaos ahead.

Funnily enough, I once used the expression when working in a tiny shoe shop on the island of Kora Kora. On one particular morning, we hadn't had any customers and I said to my boss, a small angry French woman named Mevette, that perhaps this was the calm before the storm. I was referring to the fact that we might get a sudden influx of customers at any moment, but, in a bizarre coincidence, five minutes later the island of Kora Kora was struck by a hurricane, a cyclone and a tidal wave all at once.

As Mevette and I were sifting through the wreckage of her shop after the hurricane, cyclone and tidal wave, she accused me of being an evil storm summoner and chased me down the street with one of her clogs.

Just in case I do have some supernatural ability to conjure storms I have never again used the expression the calm before the storm. But Kipp Kindle, who had never even been to Kora Kora, used the expression right at that moment.

'I hope this is not the calm before the storm,' Kipp said, as he folded the blueprint up so Cymphany could put it in her satchel.

Cymphany and Tobias looked worried—Cymphany, because she knew what the expression 'the calm before the storm' meant, and Tobias, because a storm right now would make it very difficult to get across the Misty Lake to the Huggabie Falls water plant.

They all left Felonious Dark's office and hurried down Tim Street to Misty Lake, at all times keeping an eye out for Felonious Dark, the creepy scientist and the two henchmen, and any potential approaching storm.

They found Felonious Dark's boat still tied to the Misty Lake jetty, and they leapt in and rowed it as quickly as they could to the Huggabie Falls water plant. Luckily, this boat had no leaks and the piranhas just watched them row past, with hungry but disappointed expressions on their faces.

When Kipp, Tobias and Cymphany arrived at the water plant, pulling up to the same vast metal platform they'd been on yesterday, they found it completely—and suspiciously—deserted.

'I really, really hope this is not the calm before the storm,' Kipp said, again.

Kipp, Tobias and Cymphany found a forklift, through some double doors off the platform. It held a crate of what appeared to be the last eight red cylinders of weirdness cure, because there was a label on the crate which read:

> **THE LAST EIGHT CYLINDERS**
> **OF WEIRDNESS CURE**

The keys to the forklift had, conveniently, been left in the ignition.

Kipp, Tobias and Cymphany gave each other several uneasy looks, as they drove the forklift back through the double doors to the big metal platform and unloaded the heavy cylinders.

'What now?' Tobias asked, when they were finished.

Cymphany examined the top of a canister. 'It looks like we can just twist the lids off these canisters, and'—she looked around—'then we could tip the weirdness cure down that drain.' She pointed to a nearby grate.

Kipp and Tobias agreed that down the drain was an excellent place to get rid of the awful weirdness cure, so they rolled the canisters over to the drain, unscrewed the lids one by one and poured out the green contents.

'This stuff stinks,' Cymphany said, holding her nose and screwing up her face. 'It's even worse than Mr Dark's feet.

I must point out that, once again, neither Kipp nor Tobias nor Cymphany used correct (bend at the knees) lifting techniques to lift the heavy canisters and subsequently risked back injuries.

If I had been there I would have demonstrated the correct lifting techniques but, as we've discussed previously, I am merely a storyteller with no physical presence in this book. So, yet again, I urge parents not to write in and berate me.

When the last drop of green, smelly weirdness cure was emptied out of the eighth and final canister, Kipp, Tobias and Cymphany stood back, feeling a bit confused. They should have been happy, because the weirdness cure was all gone, and they had foiled the creepy scientist's plans. But they looked at each other as if to say, surely it can't be this easy.

Tobias laughed. 'If someone were writing a book about our adventures they'd be pretty disappointed with this anti-climactic ending, wouldn't they.'

Funnily enough, there was someone writing a book about Kipp, Tobias and Cymphany's adventures, and that someone is me, and at about this point it would be appropriate to say that I am pretty disappointed with this anti-climactic ending. So disappointed, in fact, that I have currently stopped typing, have my head down and am sobbing uncontrollably into my folded arms.

A book has not had an ending this anti-climactic since the dictionary ended with the word Zulu, and I'm crying because, as a general rule, books with less climactic endings than the dictionary sell only three copies: one bought by the author, one bought by the author's mother, and one bought by a German couple who don't speak very good English and as such cannot read the warning label on the front, which says:

DO NOT BUY THIS BOOK–
anti-climactic ending contained within.
Please refer to the reference section
and read a dictionary instead.

So I was extremely relieved, and able to stop crying, when Kipp, Tobias and Cymphany received a nasty surprise.

I'm sorry to say (but not really sorry, because I will surely sell more books now) that by nasty surprise I mean the children were startled when the platform's powerful floodlights burst on.

Kipp, Tobias and Cymphany shielded their eyes and squinted through the bright haze. Standing on the far side of the platform, in front of the big double doors, with his hand on the light switch, was Felonious Dark, with the creepy scientist and the two big henchmen beside him.

'Oh dear,' exclaimed Kipp. 'I think this might be the storm.'

12

Another Chapter with Boats
But This One Also Has Ropes
and a Lot of Other Things

People might carry rope for a number of reasons. They might be keen rock climbers carrying their climbing rope in case they find a steep rock face to ascend. Or they might be rope salesmen selling the latest super strength, micro-fibre cords. But sometimes people carry ropes because they want to tie things up. And as Kipp, Tobias and Cymphany saw the coils of rope hanging over each henchman's shoulders, they suspected that the henchmen were not rock climbers or rope salesmen, which could only mean one thing.

'Oh dear,' said Kipp, as if to say, those big coils of rope look just right for tying up children.

'Oh no, you children have ruined everything,' the creepy scientist screamed.

'Oh dear,' said Felonious Dark, throwing his hands in the air dramatically. 'You children are incredible. You've foiled our plans—you've tipped away all the weirdness cure. You've saved Huggabie Falls, and there was nothing we could do to stop you.'

Unfortunately, the words of the creepy scientist and Felonious Dark did not match the triumphant tones in their voices or the smug grins on their faces.

'Quick, run,' Cymphany shouted, but no sooner had she said it than she realised the only escape was back through the platform's double doors, which were blocked by the creepy scientist, Felonious Dark and the henchmen.

Kipp, Tobias and Cymphany's eyes darted towards the boat. They obviously all had the same idea: jump back in it and row away. It was only a metre or so from them, but no one moved, as it was obvious they'd never be able to row away before Felonious Dark, with his spidery long legs and arms, bounded across the platform and jumped on the boat as well. Then they would be stuck in a boat with an evil man and water beneath them that was full of hungry piranhas, which was a scenario they already knew all too well.

Felonious Dark seemed to be enjoying himself. He took a coil of rope from one of the henchmen and moved towards the children.

Kipp, Tobias and Cymphany clung to each other, and for each step Felonious Dark took towards them, they took a corresponding step backwards away from him. This worked fine for a while, but then the children found they couldn't take any more steps backwards because they were backed up against one of the walls bordering the platform.

'If anyone has any great escape plans,' Kipp

whispered out of the corner of his mouth, 'then now would be a good time to tell the rest of us.'

Tobias looked around. To the left were giant ten-metre-high vats of water, a forklift, and crates. To the right was piranha-infested water. In front was the drain, down which they had poured the weirdness cure. And scattered around the drain were the empty weirdness-cure canisters.

'What about the forklift?' suggested Tobias, making sure to talk softly so that Felonious Dark couldn't hear him.

Cymphany shook her head. 'It's no good. No one ever made a getaway on a forklift. They don't move fast enough.'

Kipp nodded. 'Cym's right. A forklift's slow speed is probably great in a factory setting, where you don't want high-speed accidents, but it's not good for us right now.'

'What about the drain?' Tobias said. 'Could we pull off the cover and escape down the drain?'

Again Cymphany shook her head. 'It's no good. The drains are too narrow. Maybe if we were leprechauns we could fit, but not fully grown children.'

Tobias frowned. 'I think we might be trapped, I don't—'

Tobias stopped abruptly mid-sentence as he noticed something on the side of one of the giant vats. It was a little red handle with a sign above it that read:

> **RELEASE VALVE**
> **NEVER USE**

'Cymphany,' Tobias whispered. 'What do they keep in big vats in water-treatment plants?'

Cymphany glanced at the release valve and immediately knew what Tobias was planning.

'Ordinarily,' she said, 'I wouldn't recommend turning a release valve unless you are one hundred per cent sure what you are releasing, but considering the fact we are about to be captured by a very evil man and a creepy scientist, I say twist away.'

Tobias looked to Kipp.

'If you don't hurry up and twist it,' Kipp said, 'I'm going to do it myself.'

But even that plan was rapidly becoming too difficult to execute, as Felonious Dark was now only a few steps away.

'Someone will need to distract Mr Dark,' Tobias whispered. 'If he figures out too quickly what we're planning then he might be able to get to the release valve before us.'

Kipp nodded, and Cymphany and Tobias knew that Kipp was volunteering to be the distraction.

Suddenly Kipp ran in the opposite direction to the release valve, straight past the drain. He leapt over one of the upturned canisters and kept running, towards the platform's edge.

The sudden movement seemed to please Felonious Dark, as if he'd been hoping the children would try to escape. A wicked smile oozed across his face as he watched Kipp running.

As soon as Tobias and Cymphany saw Felonious Dark's wicked eyes follow Kipp, they ran for the release valve.

Kipp reached the edge of the platform and skidded to a stop. A puzzled look crossed Felonious Dark's face. He put his hands on his hips. 'Why did you bother doing that?' he said.

But before anyone could answer, the clanking of Cymphany and Tobias's feet on the metal platform caught his attention and he spun around. His eyes darted between the release valve and the running children, assessing the rapidly narrowing gap between the two.

'Oh, no you don't,' Felonious Dark growled. He dropped the heavy coil of rope he was holding and catapulted himself towards the release valve.

Felonious Dark was fast, scarily fast. But Tobias still managed to reach the valve first. Unfortunately, though, he didn't have time to turn it before he was grabbed by the back of his jumper and flung to the ground.

Cymphany tried to run past, but Felonious

twisted and hissed at her like a king cobra snake.

The violent hiss startled Cymphany so much she fell backwards and landed on her bottom with a heavy thud.

Seeing the terrified looks on the two children's faces, Felonious Dark sniggered. 'Nice try, you little fools. But you are no match for me. Did you really think you could race me to the release valve? I am too smart and too fast for you.'

'Hey,' yelled Kipp, to the accompaniment of a metallic rolling sound. Felonious Dark's eyebrows lifted a touch, and he turned around. Kipp was rolling one of the empty canisters towards him, pushing it as fast and as hard as he could.

Felonious Dark watched curiously and calmly as Kipp rolled the canister closer and closer, and then he casually lifted one of his boots and stopped it with his heel. This action brought the canister to a sudden stop, but did nothing to stop the forward momentum of Kipp, and he was catapulted somersaulting through the air.

Kipp yelped as Felonious Dark caught him by one of his ankles and held him, struggling and terrified, upside down, in the same way someone might hold a large fish they've just caught.

Felonious Dark bent over and leered at Kipp's upside-down face. 'What do you think you're doing, you silly little boy?'

'Well,' said Kipp, wriggling with the feeling of blood rushing to his head. 'I was sort of hoping the heavy canister would roll into your legs and knock you over.'

'Really?' Felonious Dark smiled. 'You children are quite stupid, aren't you? Don't you know anything about the laws of physics?'

'Of course not,' Kipp exclaimed. 'We're only in primary school.'

Felonious Dark laughed. 'Well you'd need a lot more force than that to knock me over.'

He's right you know. I mean I don't know much about the laws of physics—hence I'm a storyteller, and not a scientist—but I know enough to know that you need a much greater force than one empty rolling cylinder to bowl over a fully-grown man, even a skinny one like Felonious Dark.

'Will this do?' said Cymphany, and as she said it, Felonious Dark heard three noises. The first noise was a loud metal twisting, winding noise— if Felonious Dark had to guess he would have suggested it sounded suspiciously like a release valve being turned. The second noise was a loud groaning, pipe-straining noise, like enormous pressure about to be released. And the third noise, which quickly followed, was a monstrous rushing-water sound. This last noise was, by far, the loudest and longest of all three.

Felonious Dark only had time to thin his lips, crease his brow and say under his breath, 'This is not part of the plan,' before a super powerful jet of water cannoned into his back.

Felonious Dark instantly released Kipp's ankle, and Kipp hit the ground as Felonious Dark

was sent flying thirty metres through the air.

Felonious Dark was thrown so far that he had time to think to himself while he was up there, *Well done, Felonious, you idiot. Way to watch the release valve. Maybe if you spent a little less time trying to make witty super-villain jokes and a little more time guarding release valves you wouldn't be in this predicament right now. That metal floor down there looks rather hard. I've never been a huge fan of pain, so I doubt I'm going to enjoy the next few seconds.*

Felonious Dark soon found out that the metal floor was just as hard and painful as he expected it to be. He bounced off it, and the high-pressure blast of water pushed and rolled him along the ground, while he flailed and gargled, until he ended up in a crumpled drenched heap at the feet of the creepy scientist and the two henchmen.

The creepy scientist rolled her eyes. 'Honestly, Dark, could you get any stupider?'

Felonious Dark groaned, wondering how

many of his bones were broken.

Thirty metres away, Kipp rolled over. 'Good work, Cym,' he shouted above the roar of the high-pressure water that was gushing from the release valve.

Cymphany smiled. 'What about you, Kipp?' she yelled. 'What a brilliant plan. You knew the cylinder wouldn't knock over Mr Dark, but it would distract him just long enough for me to spin the release valve. Brilliant.'

'Yes…brilliant,' Kipp said, with the sort of bewildered tone someone might have if they are being given far, far too much credit for having any sort of brilliant plan.

Cymphany slid under the jet stream of water. 'But the creepy scientist and the henchmen are still between us and the door, and they're headed this way,' she shouted.

Kipp and Tobias turned and saw that Cymphany was right. The creepy scientist and the henchmen were marching towards them.

'No more games,' the creepy scientist roared

above the sound of the water. 'You've become an annoyance. So, unless you have any more brilliant plans I'm afraid it's curtains for you.'

I personally have never understood the phrase, 'It's curtains for you', but basically the creepy scientist was saying that the children were soon about to meet a terrible, terrible fate. And this fate was unlikely to involve curtains, or any other room furnishings, but it was more likely to involve piranhas asking for toothpicks so they could pick the little bits of children meat from between their teeth after they'd enjoyed a sumptuous three-course children meal.

At this point in the story, I must tell you I have started to become very concerned, because books that end with three children dying a gruesome and horrible death are even worse-selling books than books that have less-climactic endings than the dictionary. I am starting to worry that at this rate I could be writing the most poorly selling book in history.

*

The creepy scientist smirked—she was only about ten steps from Kipp, Tobias and Cymphany, and she was walking rapidly alongside the stream of water towards them.

'If you do happen to have a great escape plan, now would be the time to use it,' she said, as if to say, I know you haven't got one so let's just get on with all this capturing-and-feeding-you-to-the-piranhas business, shall we?

A faint voice could be heard above the roar of the water, so faint the creepy scientist had to turn her head to hear it.

The voice said, 'Will this do?'

The creepy scientist wondered about this for a second before she said to herself, 'Will what do?'

Then the creepy scientist noticed something. It was a little red thing within the jet stream of water. Or, to be more accurate, it was a little red thing that was rapidly getting bigger. Then the creepy scientist worked out it had actually been a big red thing all along that had only appeared little at first because it was a long way away.

The creepy scientist worked out exactly what the big red thing was just in time to dive to the ground as a canister—propelled by the enormous thrust of a powerful jet stream of water—rocketed past her head like a surface-to-scientist missile.

The two henchmen, who were following behind the creepy scientist, took about one second longer than the creepy scientist to work out what the big flying red thing was. It probably took them longer because they weren't quite as smart as the creepy scientist, hence they were henchmen and not creepy scientists themselves.

The canister caught both of the henchmen in their chests. There was a massive thud as they were flung backwards across the platform, colliding with the wall next to where Felonious Dark still lay in a crumpled heap. The henchmen slid to the ground, unconscious, leaving two henchmen-shaped dents in the wall. The canister rolled away, with two henchmen-shaped dents in it as well. If you put the dents in the canister and the dents in the wall together, and tipped in some plaster of Paris, you could have moulded two perfect flying-henchmen-shaped statues.

It was at about this time that the jet stream of water finally slowed down and gurgled to a stop, with all the water presumably now emptied out of the giant vat.

The creepy scientist got to her feet and turned to see that both her henchmen had been knocked out and that Felonious Dark was lying sobbing on the ground.

Kipp, Tobias and Cymphany glanced at each other—probably thinking, well, that *almost* worked perfectly. The creepy scientist stared at them. Perhaps she was trying to work out if they had any more brilliant plans.

After what seemed like an eternity, the creepy scientist laughed. 'You idiots. You may have poured away the weirdness cure, and taken out Felonious Dark and my henchmen, but won't do you any good. I've still won. We didn't need the rest of that weirdness cure anyway. There is already enough weirdness cure in the water, and now there is no stopping it. Unless you have this.' The creepy scientist removed from her pocket a small vial of purple liquid. 'This is a powerful weirdness-cure antidote. A cure for the cure, you could say. Just this little vial tipped into the town's water supply will cure everyone within hours. But without it, the effects of the weirdness cure will become permanent by morning.'

Now at this point in the story you're probably thinking the same thing I was thinking, which is if I were a super-villain, and I had a fiendish plan, which most super-villains do, then the last thing I'd do is tell the heroes *exactly* how they can foil that plan. I mean, Kipp, Tobias and Cymphany already thought they'd foiled the creepy scientist's plans, by emptying the last of the weirdness cure down the drain. And if the creepy scientist had just let them go at this point, the children would have gone home to bed and by morning the weirdness cure would have become permanent and the bad guys would have won—Huggabie Falls would have lost all its weirdness, and this book would be over. And I would have started crying again because books where the bad guys win are even less popular than books with less-climactic endings than the dictionary and books where the heroes meet a gruesome fate. I doubt I could even convince my own mother to buy a copy of a book where the bad guys win.

Now, some untrusting readers out there might again be suspicious that I am manipulating this story, in much the same way as you suspected I planted that business card in the Kindle's letterbox all those chapters ago. Your lack of faith in me upsets me, it really does. There is something known as storyteller integrity, you know, and that means never messing with the actual events of a story to make the story better.

You don't believe me?

Okay, you got me, there isn't such a thing as storyteller integrity, but, still, the fact remains that the creepy scientist was silly enough to tell the children her fiendish plan and *exactly* how they could stop it. And as Cymphany stood there looking at the defeated looks on Kipp and Tobias's faces, she realised she had to do something—she couldn't let the bad guys win.

And as the creepy scientist laughed with triumphant glee, clutching the vial of weirdness-cure antidote in her hand, Cymphany came up with her own fiendish plan.

She stepped forward. 'Well, it seems that we tried our best but we still lost,' she said.

The creepy scientist stopped laughing abruptly. 'Really? You're giving up that easily?'

'I am.' Cymphany nodded. 'But I've got one more thing to say.'

The creepy scientist paused. She couldn't see anything wrong with letting Cymphany say something—after all, she *had* won and there *was* no way they could stop her now.

Cymphany stepped towards the edge of the platform. 'I just wanted to say…'

She took another step towards the edge of the platform.

The creepy scientist hadn't worked out that she was trying to get as close to the edge of the platform as possible.

Cymphany sneakily slipped her hand into her satchel and grabbed a handful of something. 'I really want to say…' she said as she sprinkled something from her hand into the water.

'I just want to say,' she began again, 'that the capital of Denmark is Copenhagen.'

The creepy scientist chortled. 'I have to admire you, Ms Chan. Even after being defeated you're still being very brave, and still trying to be weird even though there is no hope.'

Kipp and Tobias weren't sure what Cymphany was up to. Was she really just telling the creepy scientist another one of her capital cities?

'There's just one more thing,' Cymphany said as she took a step away from the platform and towards the creepy scientist.

The creepy scientist raised her eyebrows. 'Really?' She was growing a little impatient. 'Well, what is it?'

'Would you like a chocolate-chip cookie?'

The creepy scientist blinked. 'Chocolate-chip cook—'

Before she could finish saying the word cookie, Cymphany revealed what was in her hand: crumbs of crushed up chocolate-chip cookies. And she threw the cookie crumbs all over the creepy scientist.

The creepy scientist gawked at her, stunned. 'What did you do that for, you silly girl?'

Kipp and Tobias were equally confused. They'd been defeated, and, on top of that, now they couldn't even enjoy chocolate-chip cookies on the way home.

But before they'd had time to get too upset about it, something slapped the creepy scientist on the side of her face. The creepy scientist stumbled and frowned. She looked down. A hungry piranha was flip-flopping and thrashing about on the platform. A second later, another piranha leapt out of the water and bounced off the back of the creepy scientist's head.

The creepy scientist turned, slowly, towards the water. Flying through the air, straight at her, were hundreds of frenzied piranhas, all seemingly desperate for delicious chocolate-chip cookie crumbs, and all bearing their razor sharp fangs. The creepy scientist screamed like someone who has hundreds of piranhas flying through the air towards her.

She slashed and smacked at the flying fish, but there were too many of them, and soon the creepy scientist had chomping piranhas all over her lab coat and one clamped on the end of her nose.

The creepy scientist squealed in horror. She threw away the vial of weirdness-cure antidote so she could grab the nose-clamping piranha with both hands.

The vial flew up and up, spinning over and

over in the air. Cymphany, Kipp and Tobias gasped, and all three of them ran to catch it.

Within seconds the glass vial reached the top of its arc and started to fall—downwards—towards the hard metal platform, where it would surely smash into a million pieces and the weirdness-cure antidote would be lost forever.

Kipp and Tobias had no hope of reaching the falling vial in time. But Cymphany was a number of steps closer, and she sprinted towards it, keeping her eyes locked on it.

Kipp screamed. 'She's not going to make it.'

And for a moment Cymphany didn't think she would make it either. But, at the last second, she dived and lunged. She hit the ground and slid on her tummy across the wet platform, catching the vial in her outstretched hand a centimetre above the ground.

'Got it,' she yelled triumphantly. But, unfortunately, she was still sliding, straight towards the edge of the platform, and straight towards the piranha-infested water.

'Oh, no,' Cymphany hollered—she had no time to do anything—and she slid straight over the edge.

Cymphany squeezed her eyes shut and prepared to hit the water. She waited for the splash and for the razor-sharp teeth of a thousand piranhas to bite into her poor doomed flesh.

But nothing happened.

She opened her eyes again and saw her own surprised reflection in the water just centimetres from her nose.

Cymphany looked up to see the smiling faces of Kipp and Tobias, each one holding onto one of her ankles.

'Good work, Cym,' said Kipp, as they hoisted her back onto the platform. 'You got the vial.'

'Great catch,' said Tobias.

'Thanks for catching *me*,' Cymphany said.

Tobias nodded. 'We couldn't get to the vial in time, but we got to you in time.'

'Help me, help me.' The creepy scientist shouted as she flailed about on the ground. She'd got the piranha off her nose, but she was still trying frantically to pull snapping piranhas off her now-shredded lab coat.

'You go tip the cure into the pipes, Cym,' Kipp said. 'Tobias and I will use those coils of rope to tie up the creepy scientist, the henchmen and Mr Dark.'

'Sorry, children, but I have no intention of

getting tied up, thank you,' a voice called out.

Kipp, Tobias and Cymphany turned around to see Felonious Dark leaping into their boat. He flung aside the rope that had moored the boat to the bollard on the platform and grabbed the oars. 'You may have won this battle,' he sneered, 'but one day we will meet again, and next time you won't be so lucky.'

Kipp jumped up. 'Quick! We might still be able to catch him.'

'Wait,' said Tobias. 'Leave him, there's no time. Let's just get this weirdness-cure antidote into the pipes and tie up the others.'

Felonious Dark smiled. 'Yes, yes, let me get away. Listen to your friend. He's very smart. He's always been my favourite out of the three of you.'

And Kipp and Cymphany did listen to their friend, although it pained them to watch Felonious Dark row away.

But there was no time to just stand there and watch. Cymphany ran up the metal stairs at the end of the platform and, checking the blueprint in her satchel, she quickly found the inlet valve for the town's water supply pipe. She opened the valve, gave the vial a quick kiss for luck, and tipped all the weirdness-cure antidote in.

'I just hope we're not too late,' she said, crossing her fingers.

When Cymphany came back down the metal stairs Kipp and Tobias had finished tying up the two henchmen and were busy helping the creepy scientist detach the last of the snapping piranhas from her shredded lab coat and throwing them back into the water.

The creepy scientist looked wet and exhausted, and was covered in hundreds of little piranha bites. 'This is all too much for me,' she sobbed. 'First thing tomorrow I'm handing in my resignation.'

'First thing tomorrow you'll be in jail,' said Cymphany. 'For tampering with the Huggabie Falls water supply.' She noticed the creepy scientist's shifty eyes darting from side to side.

'If you're thinking of trying to escape like Mr Dark,' she warned, 'then you'd better stop quick smart, because I've got another pocket full of crushed chocolate-chip cookies here and if I throw them over you those piranhas will be back out of the water in no time.'

That seemed to keep the creepy scientist quiet, and Kipp and Tobias quickly went about tying her up with the leftover rope.

13

A Couple of Strong Deckhands

The funny thing about water plants that are built in the middle of lakes is that you can quite easily get stuck on them if you don't have a boat. This isn't usually a problem as you need to boat to get out to the water plant in the first place so you would usually have one with you.

But if you rowed out to the water plant, and then encountered a creepy scientist, a couple of henchmen and a thin nasty man, and you were able to defeat them, but then the thin nasty man got away and stole your boat, then you'd have a severe boat-shortage problem.

'It's not a problem,' said Cymphany. 'We can use the boat the creepy scientist, Mr Dark and the henchmen used to get out here.'

But after an exhaustive search of the water plant, they couldn't find that boat anywhere.

When they asked the creepy scientist about it she shrugged. 'I don't know, that twit Dark must have stolen both boats, so we'd be trapped here,' she said.

Kipp frowned. 'He really isn't very nice, is he.'

The creepy scientist, Cymphany and Tobias all gave Kipp a look, as if to say, no, of course he isn't very nice, that much we've already established.

Five minutes later, the henchmen woke up and complained of thumping headaches.

Cymphany felt sorry for them. 'I suppose we could get them some water.'

Tobias raised his eyebrows. 'Get them water?

Cymphany, they tried to kill us!'

But it turned out the henchmen weren't really such terrible guys. They appreciated the glasses of water Cymphany brought them, and they told the children they would never have hurt them, and they didn't much like their employer, the creepy scientist, especially after they'd found out what she was up to, and they were considering a change of career. Kipp untied their hands just enough to play snap with them, which made the henchmen very happy. 'Playing snap will occupy us till morning,' Kipp said. 'When hopefully someone will come to rescue us.'

'Then we'll be able to see if the weirdness-cure antidote has worked,' said Tobias nervously.

Kipp and Cymphany were nervous too. The three children just hoped they'd poured the antidote into the water supply in time, and that everyone in town would drink the water in time.

Doctors generally advise people to drink at least eight glasses of water a day, but that doesn't mean everyone does it, especially not when there are all sorts of other things to drink, like soft drinks and hot chocolate, and especially when the hot chocolate hasn't been mixed in properly so you get lots of yummy crunchy chocolate bits on top.

The creepy scientist absolutely refused to play snap. She was still quite irritated at having her master plan foiled by three pesky children, plus, she was covered in painful piranha bites.

During the card game, which was not working as well as Kipp had hoped, as far as passing the time goes—the henchmen only knew how to play snap, and one game of snap is great, but four-hundred-and-ninety-seven games of snap in a row becomes slightly less great—Kipp said, 'Cymphany, how did you know the piranhas would jump at those chocolate-chip cookies like that?'

'Snap.' The other henchmen slammed his hand down on the table. 'No...sorry.' He frowned. 'That's a seven and an upside down two. My mistake.'

'I don't get it,' Kipp continued. 'I thought the piranhas weren't weird anymore. Choc-chip-cookie-eating piranhas sounds pretty weird to me.'

'I worked out the piranhas were still weird,' Cymphany said. 'Because they never drank the weirdness cure.'

Tobias shook his head. 'But they *live* in Misty Lake. How could they not drink the water?'

Cymphany smiled. 'Think about it. The Huggabie Falls water plant takes water from Misty Lake, treats it, and pipes it into town. The weirdness cure wasn't being put into the water until *after* it had been pumped from Misty Lake. Hence the Misty Lake water is still fine, and hence the piranhas are still weird.'

Kipp, Tobias and the henchmen all stared at Cymphany with their jaws hanging open. Even the creepy scientist looked impressed. 'You're a genius,' she said.

'When Tobias had his back pocket bitten off by that piranha,' Cymphany continued, 'I noticed he had lots of cookie crumbs in it. And I had more cookies in my satchel. It wasn't till tonight that I worked out that that was what the piranhas were after all along. So, I sprinkled some chocolate-chip-cookie crumbs in the water to get the piranhas into a feeding frenzy. After that I just hoped they'd jump at the creepy scientist when I threw the crumbs all over her.' Cymphany grinned. 'And, of course, my plan worked.'

The creepy scientist furrowed her brow. 'Wait. You guys call me the creepy scientist?'

Kipp, Tobias and Cymphany nodded.

'I always thought my nickname would be the stylishly glamorous scientist,' said the creepy scientist.

Kipp, Tobias and the henchmen agreed Cymphany's plan was an outstanding one, and they continued playing snap till morning, when they finally fell asleep.

'Ahoy there, landlubbers.'

The children were woken by a familiar voice.

'Is that...' Cymphany rubbed her sleepy eyes.

'It sounds like Mr Haurik.' Tobias yawned. An ace of hearts was stuck to his forehead.

'It is Mr Haurik,' Kipp said, pointing.

From out of the mist emerged a ship, with three masts, all rigged with billowing black sails. In the prow, with a telescope to his eye and a foot on the figurehead, was Mr Haurik. He was back in pirate clothing, complete with an eye patch, a wooden peg leg, and his trusty, yet somewhat annoying, parrot on his shoulder.

'Ahoy there, ahoy there,' the parrot shrieked as Mr Haurik pulled his ship alongside the water-plant platform, and set down a wooden plank to disembark.

'Mr Haurik, are we ever glad to see you,' Cymphany said and she ran to Mr Haurik and gave him a big bear hug.

Mr Haurik looked about. 'What are you children doing out 'ere, then?'

All speaking at once, Kipp, Tobias and Cymphany told Mr Haurik the whole story as quickly as they could.

'That be an incredible story,' said Mr Haurik. 'The 'ole town turned to scurvy normalness. It's a good thing ye children put a stop to it.'

'Well, hopefully we have,' said Cymphany. 'We've got to get back to town as quickly as possible. You seem to be okay, but we don't know about everyone else.'

'I like your new ship, Mr Haurik,' said Tobias.

'Aye,' said Mr Haurik, adjusting his eye patch. 'She be a wonderful little vessel for transportin' me caravan.'

Kipp, Tobias and Cymphany saw now that Mr Haurik's caravan had actually been built into the ship, in the spot where cabins would usually be.

'You got your caravan back.' Kipp cheered.

'Aye,' said Mr Haurik. 'I love me caravan, and me spa baths, even if they do make the old peg go a bit mouldy. And now I got this ship I can sail Misty Lake and enjoy me hot tubs at the same time.'

'Pirate ship, pirate ship,' squawked the parrot.

'Quiet, ye scoundrel,' scolded Mr Haurik. 'Curse those damn murderous scavengers o' th' seas. I don't want anybody associating me with one of those.'

Kipp, Tobias and Cymphany smiled at each other. 'Well then, buying this ship was a wonderful idea,' Tobias said, giggling. 'Especially with that black flag you've got up there with the white skull and crossbones on it.'

'You like it?' Mr Haurik beamed. 'I designed it meself. Just came up with the idea out of nowhere.' Mr Haurik seemed oblivious to the fact that his design was the international symbol for pirates.

'It's great, Mr Haurik,' said Cymphany, as if to say, Mr Haurik we don't know why you can't see that you act, talk and look exactly like a pirate, but we love you for it and it's great to have you back to your normal weirdness.

'Anyway,' said Mr Haurik, gesturing towards his ship. 'Let's get you children back to shore. Leave this scurvy bad lot tied up 'ere and I'll get in touch with the local authorities to come and pick 'em up, and look for that fiend Felonious.'

'Actually, Mr Haurik,' Cymphany whispered to Mr Haurik, 'the two henchmen are quite nice, and they're looking for a job.'

Mr Haurik smiled. 'Is that so? I could use a couple of strong deckhands for me crew.'

'Crew, crew,' the parrot squawked.

'What do ye say, lads?' Mr Haurik called out. 'Would ye join a crew that has nothing to do with pirates?'

The henchmen glanced at each other. 'Do you play snap?' one asked.

Mr Haurik threw his head back. 'Only every day and twice on Sundays. *Arrrr.*'

And that seemed to be all the convincing the henchmen needed.

Mr Haurik's new crew helped escort the creepy scientist onto the boat, and Mr Haurik sailed the children back to shore in his new pirate ship, complete with its inbuilt four-storey caravan. It was a much more enjoyable voyage on Misty Lake than the one the children had endured in Felonious Dark's boat only yesterday.

Kipp, Tobias and Cymphany returned to town, feeling nervous. Even though they'd seen that Mr Haurik was back to normal weirdness, they didn't know about everyone else.

There were some encouraging signs when they passed Tim the council worker, who was busily painting the Tim Street sign back to Digmont Drive.

When the children asked about it, Tim just shrugged. 'Oh well,' he said. 'I had a street named after me for a day. That's more than most people ever have.'

Kipp, Tobias and Cymphany smiled at each other, as that was good to see, but it didn't mean they could be sure that their families were back to normal.

With the aid of Tobias's egg timer, Kipp, Tobias and Cymphany ran all the way back to Tobias's house in exactly three minutes. They were very relieved to see wooden boards back over the windows of the Treachery house and an angry mob assembled on the front lawn.

Cymphany approached one man on the outskirts of the mob. 'What's going on?' she asked.

'It was all a lie,' the angry man said.

'Yes,' said a nearby angry woman, swinging a shopping bag full of rocks above her head. 'The Treachery family never won the lottery. They fooled us all.'

'That's too bad,' said Kipp, without meaning it one little bit.

Tobias hid behind his two friends. 'Well, it looks like things are back to normal here at least,' he whispered to Kipp and Cymphany. 'I'd better sneak around to our secret family entrance in the back and go inside. See you at school.'

A grinning Tobias gave Kipp and Cymphany a big hug and he snuck away from the angry mob and slipped down the side of the house.

Kipp turned to Cymphany. 'Well, at least the weirdness-cure antidote worked for Tobias's family.'

'That's good,' said Cymphany, as if to say, let's hope that isn't the *only* family it worked on.

Three egg-timer minutes later they were at Cymphany's house.

'I hope the weirdness-cure antidote has worked on my parents,' said Cymphany as they approached. 'The weirdness cure had the opposite effect on my family, so who knows what the antidote will do?'

Kipp shrugged. 'We'll find out soon enough.'

And they did, when they saw Mr Chan out the front dumping a box of jam in the rubbish bin.

'Hi Dad,' Cymphany shouted. 'Aren't we having jam for breakfast?'

'Yuck!' Mr Chan screwed up his face in exactly the same way Cymphany had screwed hers up earlier—screwing up faces obviously ran in the Chan family. 'Don't even mention the word jam. I'm so sick of jam that I had to quit my job at the jam factory. But in a stroke of luck my old boss rang up just now and offered me my old job back.'

Kipp and Cymphany exchanged a knowing look.

'That's good news, Mr Chan,' said Kipp.

'Are you staying for brekkie, Kipp?' Mr Chan said. 'I promise we won't be eating jam.'

'No thanks,' said Kipp anxiously. 'I've got to get home.'

Cymphany smiled, as if to say, I know how desperately you want to get home to see if your family is once again the weirdest family in all of Huggabie Falls. 'Well, go on then,' she said, after giving him a hug. But she didn't even have time to give Kipp the egg timer, as he was already halfway down the street.

Kipp had never run as fast as he did on the way to his house. He didn't even need the egg timer. By the time he arrived on his front porch his heart was thumping so hard, and so fast, that one of Kipp's neighbours actually went to the window because she thought there was a helicopter flying overhead.

Kipp almost didn't want to open the door. Sure, the weirdness-cure antidote had worked for Cymphany's family, Tobias's family and

Mr Haurik, and the street signs were back to Digmont Drive, but there was still a chance his parents hadn't drunk the antidote water in time.

With a big breath, Kipp pushed open the Kindle household's front door and stepped inside.

14

What Kipp Couldn't See

The front room of the Kindle house was empty. The television in the corner was on and Kipp's sister was watching a cartoon duck with a big mallet in its hand chase a cartoon rabbit.

'Hello,' Kipp said timidly.

Kaedy's head snapped in his direction. 'You're in big trouble,' she said, grinning.

Then Kipp caught a whiff of coffee, and a wonky pottery mug with steam wafting out the top floated across the room. Kipp instantly knew things were back to normal. He could tell from the height of the mug that it was his mother carrying it. Kipp then noticed a newspaper hovering above his father's favourite armchair, and a bottom-shaped indentation in the cushion of the chair. The hovering paper folded to one side. 'Kipp, my boy,' said his father's voice. 'Where in heaven's name have you been?'

Kipp smiled. He couldn't see his parents, which was perfect because the Kindle family was invisible. They were the only invisible family in the entire world. Kipp could see his sister, because the Kindle family's inherited invisibility didn't usually kick in until the mid-teens, so neither Kipp nor Kaedy had turned invisible yet.

Kipp was so relieved to see his parents back to normal, or to be more accurate to *not* see them back to normal. 'Mum, Dad, you're invisible again,' he said.

'Again?' His mother's voice sounded confused. Kipp could tell she was standing next to his father because the mug hovered next to his father's chair. Then the mug lifted a bit, tilted, and there was a slurping sound.

'Don't try to change the subject, Kipp Kasper Kindle,' Kipp's dad said. Kipp always knew he was in big trouble when his father used his full name. 'You disappeared in the middle of the night and you didn't tell your mother and me where you were going. Explain yourself, and tell the truth.'

'Okay,' Kipp said, and then he told his parents the whole story. He told them about Felonious Dark, about Cymphany getting turned into a baby hippopotamus, the piranhas in Misty Lake, the Huggabie Falls water plant, the creepy scientist, the henchmen, the weirdness cure, the weirdness-cure antidote—all of it. Kaedy even stopped watching her cartoon for a while to listen.

'So, in conclusion,' Kipp said, feeling like he had just told his parents a story that could easily fill a book, which of course it could—and has. 'I wasn't able to call you and tell you where I was because there were no phones at the Huggabie Falls water plant, and I know I broke a lot of rules and did a lot of wrong things, but I was only doing it to save Huggabie Falls.'

Kipp waited for a response, but no one spoke. One of the disadvantages of having invisible parents is you can't see the expressions on their faces, so you're never able to tell if they believe you or not.

But if it is possible to hear the tiny, faint skin-creasing noise of two parents raising their eyebrows at each other, Kipp could have sworn he heard it then.

He shrugged and went on. 'I always wished I wasn't from an invisible family, but after I saw you guys the other day, and I mean literally *saw* you, I realised I just wanted our family back to the way it was.'

Kipp's sister had that smile on her face, the smile that says, you're in big trouble, Kipp, and I'm loving it.

Finally, Kipp's father burst out laughing.

'One thing is for sure, son, you have a very active imagination. Your mother and I have been invisible since we met, as you yourself will be one day, and I don't believe many other parts of your story either. So you are grounded for two weeks for lying, another two weeks for making us all worry about where you went last night, and, finally, because it took your mother two hours of scrubbing to get the stench of marinated bats' tongues out of your school uniform, I'm adding a further week of grounding so you'll learn to take better care of your school clothes. So that is five weeks in total.'

'Five weeks!' Kaedy squealed with glee. 'That is a long time.'

'Hush, Kaedy,' cautioned Kipp's mother. 'Or you'll be grounded for gloating.'

But Kipp didn't mind being grounded for five weeks. Right then nothing could upset him. He was just so relieved that his family was invisible again.

'That's a fair punishment,' said Kipp, smiling

broadly. 'I'm really sorry I made you worry, and that I made up that big story. I really just went over to Tobias's house and forgot to ask, or leave a note. I'll go upstairs to my room now, if that's okay.'

Even though Kipp couldn't see his parents' faces, he could hear their stunned silence.

His sister looked shocked. She was obviously hoping for her brother to put up much more of a fight than this, which potentially could've extended his grounding.

'Ummm...' Kipp's father hesitated. 'Very well then, it's...good to hear you're sorry. Ahhh...go to your room and we'll see you for breakfast soon.'

Kipp was so happy, he almost skipped out of the room. As he went down the hall he saw the Kindle family portrait hanging on the wall. It showed him and Kaedy sitting on a bench in the middle of a park with a hat and a scarf floating beside them. Kipp lifted the portrait off the wall, held it in his hands and smiled. He knew that when the picture was taken his father was sitting to the left of him, and his mother to the right. And even though Kipp couldn't see his parents in the picture he knew they were there, and they would always be there. That was all that really mattered.

'Oh, and by the way,' Kipp's father called out. 'Your teacher, Tertunia Turgan, rang.'

'Oh, yes,' Kipp said. If there was one person the weirdness-cure antidote didn't work on, Kipp hoped it was Mrs Turgan. 'What did she want?'

'She said she was looking forward to seeing you, Cymphany and Tobias at school today. She said things were back to normal, so you'd better all bring your best running shoes to school, and stock up on bat repellent. Which is weird. I didn't think you had physical education today.'

Kipp shook his head, but he was still smiling, even though he knew he was going to spend the whole day running from Mrs Turgan, and probably trying to stop himself getting turned into a baby hippopotamus, or a pumpkin, or a toilet seat.

He hung the Kindle family portrait back on the wall, went to his room, closed the door and breathed a huge sigh of relief. Things were finally back to normal, or, to be more accurate, things were finally back to weird.

The end.
(for real this time!)

Ralph the Rat's
Portuguese to English
Translations

Bem, bem, bem, duas crianças e um hipopótamo, isso é muito estranho—
Well, well, well, two children and one hippopotamus, this is very strange.

Senhora Turgan—
Mrs Turgan.

Eu tenho medo dela, eu ficarei quieto—
I'm scared of her, I'll be quiet.

Morcegos, morcegos, morcegos, morcegos horríveis!—
Bats, bats, bats, horrible bats!

Eu concordo, que tiro preciso—
I agree, what a precise shot.

Oh, não—
Oh, no.

Book 2!

'I'm so glad everything is back to normal—or back to weird. I'd be happy if nothing else ever happened in Huggabie Falls,' said Cymphany.

Tobias nodded. 'I wouldn't worry. After the extremely weird thing that happened, I don't think anything else is going to happen for a while.'

At that exact moment, a blood-curdling scream ripped through the sanctuary. It was so loud and so forceful that it pushed Kipp, Tobias and Cymphany's fringes up, so their hair made little upright walls on top of their heads.

Find out what happens next in Huggabie Falls in *The Unbelievably Scary Thing that Happened in Huggabie Falls*, out in October 2018.